"Reality must be re-invented for each decade. With *Discontinued* Mr. Thompson has done just that. His story is at the same time mesmerizing and chilling. His style is unique, as if for the first time in years a mirror has been held up into which we must stare and see the passions and pandemoniums of our Time. Youth will read the book and see its truth, embrace its honesty without question. Without trickery or malice, *Discontinued* pulled out my old crutches about story-telling out from under me, and left me frightened, exhilarated—and healing. One hell of a book!"

—Paul Zindel

Other books by
Julian F. Thompson
A Band of Angels
A Question of Survival
Facing It
The Grounding of Group 6

point

DISCONTINUED

Julian F. Thompson

SCHOLASTIC INC.
New York Toronto London Auckland Sydney

ISBN 0-590-42464-5

12 11 10 9 8 7 6 5 4 3   1 2 3/9

Printed in the U.S.A.   01

For the beauty of hope and, always, Polly.

DISCONTINUED

1. THIS BOOK IS NOT ABOUT BASKETBALL

This book is not about basketball. It is, for example, a great deal less about basketball than *Moby Dick* is about fishing.

As a matter of fact, this book is quite a bit less about a lot of things than *Moby Dick* is. It's about some other stuff.

2. DUNCAN BANIGAN

The weather forecast on the radio the night before had called for a cloudy day with periods of April showers, and a high in the lower fifties. But on the day itself, it hadn't rained at all. There'd been some clouds, but just the nice, white, fluffy kind, and the sun had shone a lot; the temperature had risen to exactly sixty-three, by middle afternoon.

The boy this book is all about was not surprised the forecast was all wrong. The same radio station also blurted out his horoscope each morning, and its predictions/urgings seldom seemed to mesh — he was a Gemini — with things that really happened, either. At one point he wondered if horoscopes were just for adults, like Preparation H, for instance. He'd never ever known a kid with hemorrhoids.

There was also news on the radio all the time. Things like the President saying we had to spend over a trillion dollars on nuclear weapons, just so we wouldn't have to use them. Sure. Right. But — come to think of it — they paid farmers not to farm, didn't they? And tobacco growers to stay in business so people could keep on killing themselves with the stuff. He wondered if the President turned on the radio and listened to *his* morning horoscope: "Take on new responsibilities. Be more optimistic."

This same boy — the one this book is all about — was (on this fine April afternoon) moving along the sidewalk by a residential street on the edge of a small city somewhere around the forty-first parallel of latitude in the eastern United States, a city more or less the size and shape of Trenton, New Jersey, if you've ever heard of it — it doesn't matter. What does matter is that he was bouncing a basketball (although this book isn't *about* basketball) and he did that very well, using both his right hand and his left, sometimes bent way over, sometimes standing straight. He also went at different speeds, and threw in little stutter steps — forward, backward, to the sides. Between these fancy moves he'd walk awhile. And he bounced the ball in different rhythms: thump — a — thump — a — thump, and rat-tat-tat.

He had on a nubby green jacket that snapped in the front; the arms of the jacket were made of an off-white vinyl material that looked and felt like leather. On the back of the jacket were stitched twelve vinyl letters, reading QUEEN OF PEACE, but because the boy had a dark green canvas book-bag on his back, only the Q and the last E were visible. On the left front of the jacket there was sewn a small vinyl disc that looked like a basketball and the words STATE CHAMPS 1982–83. In the State Tournament program, after the boy's name, it had said: 16, Jr., 6′3″, 180.

Here's what he looked like: nice. His hair was light brown, parted a little left of center, short in the front (so it wouldn't get in his eyes when he shot the jumper), longer on top and in the back. He had blue eyes; a short, straight, solid nose; and freckles. His normal expression was cheerful and alert, like a golden retriever's, but the hair on his face was light and hard to see, not really whiskers. He thought that he looked baby-faced and immature, but college coaches paid more attention to his jaw than he did. It was that good, determined Irish jaw, with muscle bunches just below both sideburns, a real Bazooka jaw. They knew a player with a jaw like that would sacrifice his body on the court to get possession, and love to take the ball inside, and score.

His name was Duncan ("Slam Dunc") Banigan, and you may like to know that his aggression and his recklessness were all used up in basketball. His girl friend thought he was a teddy bear.

In addition to his size and basketball ability, there was one other thing that distinguished Duncan Banigan from the few other people on the street that day.

Get this: He had a tennis visor, upside down, around the very middle of his face.

His brother Brian had brought the dumb thing back from either Reno or Las Vegas just the year before, and it was red and had HARRAH'S TENNIS SHOOT-OUT printed on the front of it, in white. Brian bought it for their mom, but he had hooked it right away — she hadn't cared — and started using it in this peculiar fashion.

You get the picture, I am sure. You know a visor's sort of like a baseball cap, without the cap part, right? Well, what he did was turn it upside down and loosen up the strap in back and pull it completely down over his head to the middle of his face, and tighten it. When he had the visor on this way, he could see straight ahead all right, but if he tried to look down, all he'd see would be this slightly concave green crescent of visor underneath his nose. He not only couldn't see his feet, he also couldn't see about halfway down the block.

It was, as he had known it would be, a great way to practice his dribble. When he couldn't see the ball, he had to feel the doggone thing, and slowly learn to *know* where it was coming up. At first it was ridiculous. The ball would come down on his foot and kick away — like, jump off to the side, bouncing onto people's lawns, or out into the street. Sometimes he'd plain miss it. Talk about a person looking like a fool: He really stunk. But still he kept on doing it, except when there was snow on the sidewalk, every day, to school and back. And slowly, slowly, he got better.

The ball began to be his friend, a buddy; more and more, it got so he could count on it. The practice dribbling became enjoyable.

It was one of the few things that he did, in the course of an average day, which made complete and total sense to him (he *wanted*, yes, to do it), and which also seemed to *work*.

3. SCHOOL

At the other extreme, there was school. As you've learned already, Duncan went to one called Queen of Peace, but it could just as easily have been another one called King of War, or Southwest Central Regional, or Dovercroft Academy. School, in Duncan's mind, was like a lot of other things (weather forecasts, horoscopes, etc.): It mostly didn't work, and maybe even *couldn't* work, even if a lot of people liked to think it did. These were (mostly) parents, or employees of the Diocese or of the Board of Education. They would, of course. To Duncan, that was like some general insisting, from his air-conditioned briefing room, that the war was going "fine."

It seemed to Duncan that the only thing he'd

learned at school was School: how to win at playing this odd game. When he'd started it, he knew already how to read and memorize — and smile and keep his shirt-tail in and get along with kids and be polite to grown-ups. Playing School involved all these — it *emphasized* all these — and as he played, year after year, he practiced and refined each skill. That was how you learned to win. You learned to memorize, with *extra* care, the things that teachers thought or said were "real important." You learned that if you had a thought yourself, it wasn't smart to mention it unless it matched up really well with something that the teacher'd said already. Also — and especially at six foot three — you learned to box out underneath, to move the ball against a zone, to keep your hands up on defense, to fill the lanes (but not to over-pass), to never "waste" the basketball.

Because he'd learned to win at School so well, people there were nice to Duncan. His teachers and his guidance counselors had always told him he was "college material," but now that he was a junior, they changed that to "college-ready, already." Mr. Hagerty, his guidance counselor that year, had told him that officially: that he was now prepared to "do college," at least from an admissions point of view.

"Hey, baby — no problayma," Mr. Hagerty had said, the last time that they met.

"Waltz-time," he'd gone on, and winked. He'd been working on a style that he imagined Coach McGuire would have used, if he'd been doing Guidance. "With your grades, I could get you into *Princeton* — just for instance — even if you weren't good for twenty-three point six a game, plus fourteen boards." He much preferred giving guidance to kids like Banigan, kids who paid attention when you talked to them and didn't have a hat on, kids who you could guide and they would get somewhere. He crossed one sharply creased trouser leg above the other knee.

"What I think we ought to do," he said (and why he whispered even he was not entirely sure), "is prune your list next fall to maybe five. One Ivy, just for class, plus let's say Chapel Hill, UCLA, and Notre Dame, of course. . . ."

The story on Mr. Hagerty was meant to be that he'd busted out of seminary, partly because he'd given greater reverence to Notre Dame than to Our Lady (especially at tournament time), and mostly because of his "relationship" with Wendy Fraticelli, who he'd later married. Wendy Fraticelli Hagerty had been the school librarian at Queen of Peace for the past year-and-a-half and, as Duncan once remarked to his buddy, Ben Ramona, she'd brought about an upsurge of cultural interest unequaled since the Renaissance.

"Yeah, I got your old upsurge," Ben had answered, in his cultured way. And, not wanting Duncan to mistake his meaning, he'd bent one arm and slapped its bicep with his other hand.

"You're a class act, Ben, you know that?" Duncan'd said. He knew, and Ben knew he knew, that Ben had never gotten anywhere with anyone.

"You wanna see my library card?" asked Benny, on a roll. He grabbed his crotch. "I'd like to 'Slam Dunc' *this*," said big, bad, bestial Ben.

The "Slam-Dunc" business was a sort of cross that Duncan had to bear. It had started in the local paper, like a lot of silly, made-up things; real people only used it as a tease. *They* mostly called him Dunc — or "Bang-Bang" for another joke, sometimes.

Terry Bissonette, his girl friend, didn't like that Bang-Bang bit at all, even once he'd told her where it came from: people kidding him for taking lots of shots, in basketball. She always called him "Duncan," though it's a fact she'd said to him "Oh, Jesus," once or twice, and she had not been angry at the time. What Terry was afraid of was that if her mother — a woman with a very dirty mind — ever heard that people called her boyfriend "Bang-Bang," then she'd assume that Terry was the . . . what? *Bang-ee?* If a person was going to keep her mother under control, it was important for her mother *not* to have stuff like that to hold over a person's head. At the times when she needed it least.

4. HAPPENING

When Duncan was two blocks away from home —
still dribbling, his head straight up — he saw his
brother Brian and his mom. They came out his front
door and down the steps and crossed the sidewalk.
Brian held the door of his Trans-Am for her, and in
she got, sliding down and disappearing, smooth as
silk, as usual. Then Brian sauntered to the other side
and eased his own self in. Duncan figured he was running her downtown, or to the mall, to pick up something she forgot, or maybe cash a check. If it wasn't
something quick like that, his mother would have
driven in her Subaru, herself. Bri believed in punctu-
ality, and he — that's him and Bri — they had a very
serious appointment.

For better than a month now, every day, they'd played some games of racquetball when he got back from school. Brian never won, of course, but the points were getting better, longer — sometimes. The thing was, Brian hadn't exercised, or played a sport in — what? — two years, about. So he was out of shape. *In* shape he was not exactly dangerous, either, but so what? Bri had more their father's body: medium in size, a little narrow-shouldered, broader in the hips, with feet that angled slightly out; his body seemed to get real soft real easily, like pears. But you could say this for the guy: He always hustled. So ever since the States (which Queen of Peace had won), they'd played, and Brian said that this was just the start of it — his brand-new fitness program.

"I'm going to make this body last a lifetime," he had said, and laughed, when Duncan blurted, "But. . . ."

Brian wasn't old, just twenty-two. His hustle had turned the coaches on at Queen of Peace, and so he'd started there, in basketball, but at the college where he went he *might* have made the JV second team, at best. And Brian didn't like to sit; it wasn't in his nature. Besides, he knew he'd never make his living playing ball.

His kind of living had a "very good" in front of it, and he'd been making one the last two years, even though he'd been enrolled in college, too.

"I'm kind of a conglomerate. I like to see a lot of balls up in the air at once, and not a lot of laws about the size and shape of them," he'd said to Duncan just the month before. "Supply-Demand and Gravity are plenty. Of course there is some risk. That's part of anything with big-reward potential. Here's the way I see it: I don't mind taking *trips* into the jungle, as long as I can live on Easy Street."

When Duncan Banigan was still a block away, Brian's clean and manicured right hand reached out and turned the key in his Trans-Am's ignition. After that, he never did another thing; in fact, in just a second's time there wasn't any "he" to do things — not that anyone could recognize, identify. The current in the car's ignition had set off a non-nuclear explosive device that simply blew his mother and himself to anything you want to call it (one big plastic bag-ful), partially destroyed two other cars, and made a gaping crater in the street.

They used a lot of excess gelignite to discontinue Brian's kind of living.

"Amateurs." So said Sergeant Hamill of the Bomb Squad (State Police) to Trooper Giambelluca, just assigned as his assistant. "They always think that more is better, right?"

Trooper Giambelluca nodded; that was what you did if you were smart. But still — he'd always thought that more was better, too.

Duncan started running right away, the visor upside down around his face, the ball still bounding from the pavement to his hand, as if it had a big elastic on it. The noise of the explosion filled his head and went along with him; he kept on seeing flash and smoke, his balance seemed real funny.

He never knew that he was yelling — nothing, names — as he was running toward the burning car. Slowly, in his mind, the words "This can't be happening to me" came up, followed by the words "Of course it is."

5. THE LATE RUTH BANIGAN

The late Ruth Banigan, Duncan's mother, had once been a sergeant in the Air Force, stationed in West Germany. And just in case you wondered: Yes, her eyes were pretty much the color of her uniform.

She'd married Gerry Banigan five years before she enlisted, and eight years before he got the largest desk in the Holiday Inn outside of Toledo, Ohio — which made him "Mr. Banigan" to everyone who worked there. Brian had been born in Stockbridge, Massachussetts, when his father was still "Gerald" and worked at a Stouffer's.

Other women often didn't understand it, but Ruth was not in love with being kept in inns. She didn't have to cook or clean, but then she hadn't planned to, ever, as a full-time thing; she also hated daytime tube, and tourists, and Toledo as a goal in life. So one fine, super-busy, crowning-glory-of-the-summer Labor Day, she'd run away and joined the Air Force. Because she knew her mother would cooperate, and thought that it was better ("only fair"), she'd taken little Brian with her. That mother, Verna, didn't like her much, and never had, but she was also bored and mad (she thought) for little-boy-Brian. Wherever Ruth was sent, at home or overseas, Verna went along and rented an apartment right nearby the base that she could fill with souvenirs and bargains from the Post Exchange. Her husband, Lou, had been taken with a fatal heart attack on the floor of the Ford plant in Mahwah, and then been caught in a machine; the benefits that stemmed from those events were just immense, forever.

"The Japs have nothing like it, I can promise you," she told her friends, delightedly. You can take your guess about Lou's feelings, same as I can.

Ruth was very pretty — gorgeously blue-eyed, and tall and slender and athletic, too (*lissome* was a word that went with her, just fine). Her look was sleek and modern, she turned heads in hangars and in offices, in lobbies and at poolside. So Gerry Banigan was very loath to lose her. He flew to Germany whenever he was able to and tried a lot of strategies to hold up the divorce. And Ruth would *almost* change her mind; at times, it seemed that he would finally get his way. As Verna often said, "The man has lovely manners, and a closet-ful of class."

In fact, he got his way sufficiently, one time, to

bring about another child's conception. That's what Ruth insisted, anyway. Brian at the age of twelve had once told Duncan, six, a slightly different story: that Duncan's father was "some mean old Kraut," and not G. Banigan at all. Duncan screamed so loud that Brian took it back, and later always swore that he'd been kidding — all right, *lying* — just to get a rise from bratty-baby-brother. Gerry wasn't absolutely certain either way, but finally made a deal with Ruth: Duncan would be his, a Banigan (uncontested and un*test*ed, too), except in terms of child support.

Duncan never knew that part of it. What he knew was Brian hadn't *looked* like he was lying when he'd told him that his father was some German. And, after the Vietnam War, a lot of stories in the paper and in different magazines had made it pretty clear to him that when American troops are stationed overseas for any length of time, they're apt to have relations with the locals.

But none of that had anything to do with Ruth Banigan's untimely death at the age of forty-two. Gerald Banigan hadn't come east and blown his ex-wife up, and neither had some mysterious German jetted in on Lufthansa for the purpose of killing the mother of his illegitimate (but athletic) child.

Ruth Banigan died for the same unreason that a lot of us will: She had some damn bad luck.

6. LOOSE ENDS

Within minutes of the explosion, the road outside of Duncan's house was full of vehicles with growling sirens, double-blinking roof lights: blue and red and yellow. And for quite a while afterwards the sidewalks and the street were thick with overweight local police officers, most of whom had never seen a thing like that before, and so said, "Holy *shit*!" and shook their heads, and hitched up on their belts.

About an hour later, tight-lipped troopers from the State Police had also made the scene, but still, between the time *they* left and Detective Lieutenant Arthur Grunfeld came, with two assistants, Duncan had a chance to go through Brian's room.

It's hard to say if he was in a state of shock or what.

At times, he felt hysterical — gulping, crying, making little hurting sounds and snuffles. Then, for a while, he'd be completely dry-eyed, concentrating, listening for any sort of sound outside, simply in a tearing hurry. "Oh my God" is what he said, a lot. When he got finished, he was satisfied; he'd done a pretty thorough job. He lay down on his bed awhile.

There wasn't much to find; he didn't think there would be: Bri was very cautious. Any records that he kept would probably have been inside his fat breast-pocket wallet. He took that wallet everywhere, even into racquetball, so now it was a part of all the processed *stuff* within, around the ruin of the smoking ex-Trans-Am.

There wasn't any money anywhere, other than the quarter, dime, two pennies in a saucer on the dresser top. Duncan always guessed that Brian must have kept a lot of cash on hand, but if he had, he'd kept it in the wallet, too. There wasn't any checkbook, either.

Inside the bottom dresser drawer, however, underneath the left-hand pile of sweaters and on top of last month's *Penthouse* there was . . . something. Something meant for him. Some years before, his brother'd told him where he kept his magazines and said that he could read them if he put them back and stayed the hell away from other stuff of his. Duncan promised, and Bri would sometimes leave him other stuff — surprises — in that drawer: riddles and cartoons, two Trojan prophylactics.

This thing was an envelope. On the outside of it Bri had printed: TO BE OPENED IN THE <u>ABSOLUTELY</u> UNLIKELY AND <u>IMPLAUSIBLE</u>

EVENT. . . . He liked to talk to Duncan just like that.

Inside, there was this one tiny slip of real thin paper, like half a rolling paper, maybe. On it were these words, in Brian's smallest script:

"*Du-du, check this out: fetish, swillys, boobytune.*"

Duncan folded it until it almost disappeared and stuck it in his wallet. The envelope he kept, and threw away downtown, days later.

When Lieutenant Grunfeld and the other plain-clothes cops arrived, Duncan was sitting at the kitchen table with the neighbor, who had also been his mother's closest friend. Mrs. Dorothy Michalis. He felt dried out and really wired. Verna Williams, his grandmother, was en route from North Jersey; Gerry Banigan would fly in from Toledo in the morning. As if things weren't bad enough already.

Ruth and Gerry were divorced when Duncan had just turned two; he hadn't seen the guy a whole lot since, nowhere near enough to feel relaxed with him, to have, let's say, a set of private jokes to shorten up and warm the space between them. His father was a dapper stranger, a source of plastic Jeeps and soccer balls and scarves, always with a card that said "Love, Dad," but nothing else, sometimes in a new and different handwriting. Any actor could have done the part (so Duncan thought) and done it more convincingly. Brian use to say he loved his father, lots, but Duncan thought he might be showing off.

Verna Williams he knew much, much better. Groan. She'd almost brought him up when he was little, teaching him the mechanics of life, like how to use the toilet paper properly and where to put your juice glass when it's empty, but she'd never really cared for him. She wasn't lilac-scented, flour-to-the-elbow, grand-maternal-minded. She'd had a crush on Bri until he'd learned to answer back and talk a little dirty, at which point he became — like almost every clerk and taxi driver — just another person she disliked. Duncan never got her real excited either way. He always felt she treated him the way a lot of people treat tropical fish, or turtles: something alive that you happened to have around.

Lieutenant Grunfeld was a total stranger. Going by his looks alone, he could have been a social studies teacher, or a mediocre ref — ten pounds overweight and used to telling people what the story was, and jokes that weren't very funny. Now he called his little class to order, getting names, addresses, times, and places, clear. Then he looked at Mrs. M. and said:

"Is there some place me and Duncan might sit down and have a little chat?"

Lieutenant Grunfeld knew a lot of things *for sure*, including this: In any scene where there's an adult and a kid, the adult must be *totally* in charge.

"Sure," said Duncan, getting up and heading for the living room.

Behind him, Grunfeld tried to score politeness points. "No," Duncan heard him say. "No, just the boy. My men will start upstairs, if that's all right." And: "Thank you *very* much. For all you're doing."

Duncan waited, standing, in the living room.

Grunfeld chose the couch, so Duncan took the rocker. The lieutenant made adjustments in his trousers, opened a notebook, very slowly, rested it along one thigh.

He *is* a tuna, Duncan thought; he really has gross thighs. German-Grunfeld thighs, detective-notebook thighs. They're *king*-thize, Duncan thought, feeling slightly crazy. He wasn't going to start the conversation, though.

Lieutenant Grunfeld finally did. "Was you and Brian what you might call *close*?" he asked. He used the really friendly voice he'd practiced off and on for years on Phil and Seth, his sister's kids, who loathed him.

"Well" — Duncan shrugged — "you know that he was six years older, right?"

Bri had checked him out on this a dozen times or more, so Duncan knew that he could do it in his sleep. Of course they hadn't figured — either he or Brian — that Brian would be dead. Dead was not in Brian's plans at all. Go-getters didn't die, they went and got. "Rich" for one, but also other things.

"It's better than a thousand-to-one shot," Bri had said. "The law enforcement people know I'm not the type for trouble. They know I vote Republican. I make no secret of where I stand on school prayer and the death penalty. And if everybody did in their sex life what I do in my business life, there wouldn't be a need to have abortions. I take precautions — plus," he'd said.

"But *if* they ever picked me up — for questioning,

let's say — they'd maybe want to talk with you as well," said Brian. "And if they ever do, your act is absolute and total ignorance." He'd smoothed his short brown hair; he smelled, as usual, of after-shave; he'd punched his brother on the shoulder, only lightly. "You'll be perfect." He'd chuckled over that one.

Then, holding up one finger in this proper-professorial routine of his: "You've never had the slightest clue as to where my money comes from, other than 'investments'; any time you asked, I said I'd made some wise *investments*. Drugs?" He'd added one more finger, up. " 'Impossible,' you say. 'My brother doesn't even drink, except a glass of wine with dinner, sometimes. He always tells me if I ever get near drugs, he'll kick my ass.' " Though that last part was true, Duncan almost had to crack a smile; in the kind of shape he was in, Brian might not have been able to get his foot up that high.

Brian then had let his fingers drop, leaving just his slightly chubby fist. "When talking to the cops, it's always best to keep your story simple and tell the truth — except not all of it. Here is what you sing, your glad refrain: 'Sir, I just don't know a thing about it.' "

If it could be said that Lieutenant Grunfeld started out fishing with little delicate dry flies, dressed with lots of sympathy, it might also be maintained that before he was done he'd worked his way up to something on the order of one of those World War I type cannons on a flatbed railroad car, like the Germans used to shoot at Paris with. It got pretty gross.

"Those son-of-a-bitches turned your mother into sausage meat and splatter, son" — Grunfeld now was leaning forward in his chair, and sweating — "but who they *thought* they'd have there sitting next to Brian, was yours *truly*."

He jabbed a thumb at Duncan, just making sure the kid had got this . . . well, rather *uptown* turn of phrase. Duncan was glad for the signal; for a second there, he really had thought that Grunfeld thought that Brian's killer thought that Grunfeld would be sitting next to Brian.

"You say that you don't know a thing about it, and I'm not calling you a liar," Grunfeld said. "Not yet, anyway. But I will tell you this. I'm plenty fucking dubious, you get my meaning? Like not at all convinced, like doubtful Thomas. And this is something else you better know, old pal-o-mine. The fellas that just orphaned you, they do not like loose ends. Tomorrow, in the paper, they'll find out they got one, maybe: you. So if I were you, I'd keep my loose end in my pants and walk away from the buildings and under the street lights, if you follow me."

He winked and nodded, standing up and pocketing his notebook.

"And if you happen to, like, suddenly recall. . . ."

Duncan took the card Lieutenant Grunfeld offered him and put it in his wallet, too. Grunfeld went upstairs to join the gentlemen in Brian's room.

Duncan passed through the kitchen on his way outside. Mrs. Michalis looked up at him as he went by, and he saw that she was crying.

He just stood in the backyard, over behind the garage where they used to put the grill sometimes in the summer. Grunfeld had made him angry, and so he'd toughed it out with him, denied him everything. It was almost like a game. But now he wasn't angry any more. He just felt overmatched.

7. WARNING

The next few chapters are going to have a lot to do with things like funerals, and the kind of crowd they attract, and different people's reactions to death, so if you really don't like to think about such matters, feel free to skip ahead.

But before you do, consider this: We all have to deal with death, one way or another, and most of us have to deal with it as a member of the audience, or even as an usher, before we get to play the lead. It doesn't hurt to know as much as possible about what you may be getting into.

Oh, and don't worry; this book isn't about death any more than it is about basketball.

8. CHOICES

"*This* is nice."

Verna Williams, Duncan's grandmother, sunk her hand into the salmon-colored, quilted, one-hundred-percent acrylic lining of the very stylish, almost *streamlined* (she might say) black casket. They were upstairs at Delaney's Funeral Home. The handles, Verna noticed, were, like, *recessed* into the sides of the casket, so as not to interrupt the clean, modern line.

"What do you think, Dunc?" she asked. She had decided to pretend to consult him about everything, treat him like the man, but her tone gave her away. She was talking to herself.

"It wasn't one of her colors, of course," she said,

still fingering the material. "Not with those eyes of hers." She was totally ignoring Gerry Banigan, Brian's father and probably Duncan's, too, for all she knew, but she had noticed his suit, an elegant double-breasted charcoal gray with just a shadow of a pin-stripe.

"But under the circumstances. . . ." She shrugged and looked directly at the boy, at last.

"Would Mother like this?" she asked him.

Duncan closed his eyes and swallowed noisily, then dropped his head a bit. His grandmother took that for a nod, agreement, and she started slowly down the aisles, glancing at the other caskets, making double-sure she hadn't missed an even better bet. She hadn't always shared Ruth's taste — and that's for sure — but the black casket seemed like a reasonable compromise. Verna Williams happened to look ravishing in salmon.

"Now how about this for Brian?" she said.

The wood on "this" was rich and lustrous brown, the handles gleaming brass.

9. FEELINGS

"It's all so weird," said Duncan. An hour before, he'd taken refuge in his room and was lying on his bed with his hands folded behind his head. His girl friend, Terry Bissonette, was sitting on the edge of the broken recliner he'd inherited from the family room downstairs.

"Unbelievable," said Terry. And when he didn't say anything else right away, she added, "Such an incredible waste."

She felt about twenty-five years old, when she said that, and also like a jerk. There were these formula things that people said after other people died, and when you couldn't think of anything else to say, you said them. And you felt like a jerk. The night before, desperate for something to *do*, she'd given herself a perm, so her hair looked just like Linda Ronstadt's, and she didn't much like that, either. Then today she'd put a skirt on to come over, and there was Duncan wearing blue jeans, as if it was a Saturday, or after school. She'd had to ask herself what she'd expected him to be wearing. A blue suit?

"I don't mean that," said Duncan. "I mean I haven't got the slightest idea how they're *feeling*, so I don't even know whether I should feel sorry for them, or what. Maybe I ought to be jealous of them, I don't know."

"I don't think you ought to be jealous of them," Terry said. "That sounds too much like wishing you were dead, you know?"

He nodded. He didn't feel that way. It had been a sort of a dramatic thing to say, and he'd thought of it, so he'd said it. He liked being there in his room with no one but Terry. The talking was superfluous. What mattered was her. She would be the only one who really understood. If there was one thing in this world that worked, it was him and her.

She was feeling a little confused, wanting so much to be *useful* — knowing him so well, but still not knowing death, and what to do with it.

Before, he'd been sitting on the bed and had said something about the funeral home, and then started pounding his fists on his knees and crying, saying a lot of wild things. She'd simply gotten up and gone over and put her arms around him, and they'd sort of flopped over onto the bed, and eventually, when he'd run out of things to say, they'd started kissing, and she had felt him getting, like, *excited*. She hadn't known what she should do. There had been a couple of deaths in *her* family already, and afterwards there seemed to be a lot of blame flying around — who'd said what, done what, and shouldn't have.

What she'd ended up doing was nothing. Just being, staying, with him. After a while, she'd gotten up and gone back to the recliner. Her skirt was wrinkled, but she didn't care.

"I guess when I was crying, I was mostly feeling sorry for myself," he said. "Because I miss them both so much, already."

"I can see that you would," Terry said. "And I don't blame you. My God, when you think about it, you've been with them almost every day of your entire life. You knew them better than any other people in the whole world, and vice-versa. I'd feel sorry for *myself*, too; I'd be a mess."

She said that seriously, but then she had to smile, inside. She'd just thought of a couple of ways he knew *her* better than he'd known them, and vice-versa, too.

Terry shook her head and squeezed her folded hands between her knees. What was the matter with her, thinking a thing like that, at a time like this? She'd always accused her mother of having the dirty mind. Not that what she was thinking was dirty, just maybe out of place.

That was the trouble when someone died; there didn't seem to be anything *in* place.

10. HOME SWEET HOME

When it came time to make plans for the reception, to be held at the Delaney Funeral Home the night before cremation and interment, Gerry Banigan had modestly stepped forward.

"Let me" — he'd put just fingertips on Verna William's elbow — "I've had experience," he said.

He'd arched his eyebrows once, at Duncan, who quickly nodded back. He didn't care who called the shots; anyone who wasn't him was fine with him. What did *he* know? Nothing; get it over with. His mood swung back and forth from rage to desolation — pessimism. Fear. He hadn't felt so young in years.

Verna hadn't argued either. For one thing, Banigan

did have the experience, reception-wise. Maybe not a lot with funerals, specifically, but certainly with, well, *events* that wouldn't be so different: sales and corporation meetings, meditation groups, bar mitzvahs maybe. Plus, two, it was his son, and his ex-wife, regardless of the fact he hadn't seen them much, for years; it was only fair to let him play some part in all of this. Besides, the man had taste — *gentility*, you might say, even.

Later, she admitted he'd done well. The evening, she informed her friends at home, went perfectly. "Ruth, she would have loved it," Verna Williams said.

Duncan was informed he had to be there early. That was just "the way it worked," they told him — and the choice of words had made him feel like puking. No matter what happened to a person, no matter what degree of chaos was going on at any given time, there was always some idiot acting as if he knew exactly what should happen next, that it "worked" this way or that. It was fucking ridiculous, Duncan thought. He couldn't see why everyone didn't realize nothing hardly ever worked, and stop pretending otherwise. But people like his grandmother didn't even look as if they were pretending. They acted completely sure. "The family," they said, arrived *at least* a half an hour earlier than what the paper said. Always. He wondered what they'd say if he told them he wanted to get there twenty minutes early and let Terry receive alongside him. Or sitting on his shoulders, maybe. Probably they'd say, "Oh, no.

That wouldn't *work* at all." It was all so totally absurd.

"Don't you have a darker suit than *that*?" his grandmother'd asked him, when he came downstairs in the tan and only one that fit him.

When their little group arrived inside the funeral home, Duncan took one look around and wanted to be somewhere else, at once. The large reception room was set up so that your eyes were drawn, whether you liked it or not, to the two caskets: the sleek modern black one and the ruggedly masculine brown one, side by side on special stands, both banked with different sorts of flowers (delicate and hardy, left to right), both indirectly but distinctly bathed in lustrous yellow light. And much too near to them were placed three leather-cushioned captain's chairs; that was where "the family" would stand (or sit, if overcome by grief, fatigue, or boredom, he supposed) while "the public" filed on by and paid "respects."

At the far end of the room there were three buffet tables covered with white cloths, and even as they entered, solemn, balding youngish men in very dark blue suits were starting to arrange the food and drink on them. Duncan thought there must be some mistake. Was this a funeral, or the Middle Atlantic States Eating Olympics? There was what looked like a smoked turkey, a whole huge ham, plus those setups for a number of hot dishes, and a bunch of different kinds of bread and rolls and salads. Another table was set up for drinks, both hot and cold, and underneath it there were a couple of extra cases of liquor, for God's sake. The third, he guessed, would start to grow desserts before too long. Maybe like a cake, with frosting: white and pink and blue, with "Happy Heaven, Ruth and Brian" on it — wouldn't that be great?

"Mmm," said Verna as she chose, and ate, an olive. She moved two others on the plate, to cover up the empty space. "Very nice, indeed."

Gerry smiled and dropped his eyes and tilted slightly forward from the waist. He always took a healthy pride in his "arrangements."

As people started to arrive, Duncan got another jolt. Apparently he had a part — a speaking role — in the proceedings. No one coming in had ever *seen* his father, and very few of them had met his mother's mother. And so, the man in charge — Delaney? — said he had to be the first one in the receiving line and introduce the people, each of them in turn, to Verna Williams on his right.

Sample:

"Duncan. Oh, my God, you poor kid. What a terrible terrible thing! We're so incredibly sorry, really we are. If there's anything — *anything* — we can do — and that goes for Joe and Patricia and Ernest, too — you just give us a call and we'll. . . ."

"Yes. Thanks a lot. Grandma, this is Mrs. Frederici, and Mr. Frederici, and — uh — Patsy and Ernie. . . ."

A few of those and he was hating the whole thing so much he actually thought he might pass out; he hadn't eaten, really, all day long. He reached, head down, for one more hand, and heard: "Look, Duncan — *I* can do this part. And you could walk around and talk to people, see your friends."

His savior: Mrs. Michalis, the good neighbor. She squeezed his hand and nodded, more or less for emphasis, and leaning, kissed him on the cheek. He felt like bawling, but he smiled instead, and fled. About a half a minute later, somewhat to his own horror, he was putting together an enormous ham and cheese sandwich, slathered with mustard, on the dark rye bread.

Ben Ramona sidled up to him. Ben had been terrific ever since it happened. Not that he wasn't always a good friend, but lately he'd been just the greatest, perfect. Duncan realized that, unlike most people, Ben had kept on treating him the exact same way he always did. He was either completely unconscious (Duncan thought) or about the most sensitive person you could ask for. It was hard to be completely sure, with Ben.

"Trust you to find the food, right off," said Ben. He squirmed inside his tie and jacket, scratched himself. "I wanted to ask you something. I hope you don't mind. But when they cremate someone, do they burn the whole coffin? Or would they take the person out first, and just do, like, *him* — the body?"

They were standing with their backs to the caskets, over near the buffet tables. Duncan still didn't like staring at the two boxes, but he was getting slightly used to being in the room with them. He'd wondered if there was anything inside them at all. In one way, it was better that his mother and his brother had been blown up, because at least he didn't have to imagine them lying there looking sort of as if they were asleep, or however they'd look.

"How should I know?" he said to Ben. "You're gross, you know that?" But he found he didn't mind talking about it that much. "I think they burn the coffin, too," he said. "It seems like a rip-off, when you first think about it, but I guess it makes sense. I mean, once you put a body into one, who else would want it?" It was actually good, for some weird reason, to talk about coffins and bodies, use the words. "Like Terry told me some stores won't take a bathing suit back. Once you've had it on, you own it."

Ben nodded. "Yeah," he said. "I heard that. And you never do see an ad for a secondhand coffin, either. Not that I ever looked." He gazed around the room. "I'd sure hate to work here, you know that?" he said. "But my mother's ten times worse than me. She told me to give you her regrets, by the way. I guess she was afraid she'd do something like the last time. I never told you, I don't think. She went to old Mrs. Pinkney's wake, right? And it was open casket? So guess what Mom did, when they had the people file by the coffin. Took one look and blew a lunch. All over the old lady. I mean, I suppose it didn't make a whole lot of difference, the lady being dead and all. But still. Dad was so embarrassed he just about shit, he told me."

Duncan shook his head and almost laughed. But then he saw Mr. Mitchell, the contractor who'd done the renovations on his house the year before, looking at him in a really solemn, sympathetic way. Mr. Mitchell was a good guy, but he still might not understand if he saw him laughing. Mom and Brian would understand, Duncan thought, but they didn't count any more. It was *their* funeral, but he had to please a bunch of other people, now. That's the way it "works," thought Duncan. Probably most people would like seeing him the way he'd been the day before, alone with Terry. The worse he'd seem to feel, the better they'd like it, probably. The better they'd like *him*. How crazy all this is, he thought.

He'd been pretty crazy himself, yesterday — crying and moaning and carrying on, and yelling about how much he *hated* losing them. He'd gotten into hating whoever'd done it, too, and the anger hadn't gone away but only settled down, the way a fire settles. He wasn't going to make it blaze up now, to please a lot of strangers. He didn't have that kind of hotdog in him; anyone who'd seen him play knew that. Yesterday was *then*. He'd been a real big baby for the longest time, but that was just with Terry and she'd said it was all right, and he'd known that it was, and afterwards he'd felt different and better, just the way you hear that people always do. A girl — a woman — *understood* the way a person felt; with a woman you didn't have to put on any sort of act.

All that had happened on the day before. Now here was Terry, once again, coming up to him and Ben.

"Boy, is this place getting packed," she said. She put a hand on Duncan's arm, as if to show him he was still connected, still a part of something. "Have you decided about the house and all?" she asked. Terry liked to organize, to have things settled. He felt anchored by her in the best ways.

Duncan shook his head. It was impossible to think of himself, still two months short of seventeen years old, as owning his own home. That was just one thing he couldn't think about.

And now another hand, this one on his shoulder, from behind; he turned around. He'd never seen this guy before: maybe middle twenties, with frizzy hair about to his shoulders, parted in the middle, and a long, blue fitted overcoat, buttoned all the way up to his neck. The guy reached out; he wanted to clasp hands — not shake, but clasp, with elbows down, like arm wrestling. His eyes were glisten-y.

"Your brother, man," he said. "He died for his religion. There ain't no greater love than that, no shit." The guy gave one more pump to Duncan's hand. "I'll be in touch," he promised, and he turned abruptly, walked away.

"Jesus, who was that?" asked Terry. She could have been a little hurt that Duncan hadn't talked to her about why anyone would want to do a thing like that to Brian, blow him up. Maybe he just thought she knew; he didn't have to say.

Duncan shook his head and shrugged. He wasn't about to start getting into that stuff with her and Ben, at that point. Maybe later, sometime. In soap operas, people always said that nothing was the same after such-and-such happened. Well, in this case, it was simple fact: Nothing would be the same. But how would it be? He couldn't begin to imagine, not at all.

There were now a lot of people in the room he didn't think he'd ever met. Terry'd wandered off some place, and he and Ben still stood there. Five fat men with highball glasses wrapped in paper napkins were arguing about "George and Billy" in front of the buffet; one of them just might have been the guy who came to fix his mother's washer-dryer; before, he'd always had a cap on. Farther off, there was a small Spanish-looking dude in a chalk-striped blue suit with big padded shoulders, and a corner of his lower lip in his teeth. Duncan pointed him out to Ben, but before he could even ask him who he was, the little man turned and wriggled through the crowd and disappeared. His name was Mister Carlo, but Ben would not have known that, either.

"And get a load of them two doozies." Being cool, Ben pointed with his eyeballs and a little sideways nod. To look at them, you'd think they'd just come from the barber shop. Black, perfect high-gloss hair (razor-cut and blow-dried), real close shaves, plus gleaming shines and matching belted raincoats. When Duncan looked at them, they stared straight back and didn't change expression in the slightest. They could have been detectives, or the Mafia. In fact, they owned a florist's shop.

Terry came back with eclairs on a plate. Ben helped himself and started making sounds — ecstatic sounds, you might say. Terry figured he was praising the cuisine, indulging in a minor sugar fit, but Duncan knew what he was hearing. Ben was making the noises that he thought he'd make, if ever he made out with anyone.

And sure enough, coming toward them through the crowd was Wendy Fraticelli Hagerty.

11. WANTING

Do you remember exactly when you stopped worrying about whether your parents really wanted you?

Maybe you're like this one person I know who never did worry about that. Or maybe you haven't stopped yet, and you're a hundred and eight. But for most people the correct answer is probably "No, not exactly," or "In junior high, I guess."

What happens in the majority of cases is that the worry's just a fleeting one (at worst) and it gets phased out, replaced by other almost opposite concerns. Such as: Will there ever be a day when They Get Off My (aching) Back? Somewhat like children in the old days, being wanted seems to be best when it is *seen* (in small services performed) and not *heard* (as in the case of nagging).

Duncan had been spared that worry. Although his father never was a factor in his life, and his mother (like *her* mother) was a less than classic "mom," he always knew she wanted him — was pleased that he existed, and was hers. He, for his part, thought that she was cool (the good kind), and that he was very lucky to be loved so sweetly, undemandingly, offhandedly.

All this made his present situation — two days after her and Brian's death — all the more unbearable. He had to face the fact that he was still a kid, in terms of knowing things that grown-ups knew. He'd always figured he had lots of time to find out what makes the guy come with the heating oil, or how you pay your taxes, or who would know the most about "investments." There wasn't any rush to learn all that. Or to find out when a person needs to get a lawyer.

Duncan thought Lieutenant Grunfeld was a jerk, but maybe he would have to deal with other cops who weren't. Should he — maybe — talk the whole thing over with some lawyer? Maybe Bri's advice — the total ignorance approach — made sense if Bri was still alive and being questioned by the cops himself. But now, with Brian dead? And how about his brother's message? Should he maybe give it to the cops? But the thing had been specifically addressed to him. Was what Brian wanted him to go and do — "check out" — for Brian's sake, or his? Was Brian fingering his murderer, or telling Duncan where he maybe ought to split to, just in case — as Grunfeld said — some people planned to kill him, too? Does a person ask a lawyer all this kind of stuff?

He didn't know. And more than that, he realized, he now had no one he could ask. No one had that role in life, that function. Sure, he had a grandma (of a sort) and other relatives (none close), but there wasn't anybody left who *wanted* him, in the sense of wanting — being willing, happy — to take care of him, or if not *him*, at least these strange new needs of his. What he had with Terry — *their* sort of wanting — was a different kind of thing, and in the long run much, much more important. But the last thing in the world he'd ever do was get her any more involved in all this killing stuff, or anything to do with Brian's "business."

He'd known that one day this was going to happen: that he'd no longer be a kid. That he wouldn't always write his mother's name along the line that asked who should be called in an emergency. That someday *he* would be this mother-father figure at the head of things, the take-charge person. Was he that already, now? He guessed he might be, even if he didn't feel like it. In basketball, when the game was on the line — his team behind by two, or maybe tied — well, then he *liked* to have the ball. To be the person called in that emergency. So, how about in life?

He didn't know. How could he? How would a person ever know? Just by doing it, he guessed.

Lying in his bed at night, those thoughts had made him take deep breaths and flex his shoulder muscles, pull the blankets and roll over on his other side.

12. REPRIEVE

Underneath the kitchen table, Duncan had his big hands spread out on his denimed thighs, and from time to time he'd run them up a ways, as far as to his knees, and back. His mother and his brother had been buried for a day, already.

"If only my apartment were *bigger*," his grandmother had said, for openers, "there wouldn't be any problem *at all*." She'd looked at Mrs. Michalis when she'd said that, speaking woman to woman. "A teen-aged boy *must* have his privacy." She'd nodded.

Now, a good bit later, Duncan said, "What I don't understand is this: Does Mom's will say that I . . . that you and I . . . *we* have to live together?"

Verna Williams sighed and made a little fanning

motion with her hand, as if there were mosquitoes in the room. "Well, no," she said. "Of course not. But as your *guardian*, you see, I'm . . . well, *responsible*. In the same sense that your mother was. And that, of course, means food and shelter — *supervision*. Right up until your eighteenth birthday." And she sighed again.

They'd been on the subject for a half an hour now. These were the facts, as Duncan understood them:

One, his mother's will had appointed *Brian* to be Duncan's guardian, in the event of her death. His grandmother was just a backup, in the event of any "unwillingness or incapacity" on Brian's part. Like being trashed in the front seat of his car, just for instance.

Two, his grandmother's apartment was too small for him to live in, and she seemed not about to move, for a variety of reasons. First, she probably wouldn't be able to find anything suitable up around where she lived, because of this incredible apartment shortage they were having there. *And*, what would she do with a place that big when he went off to college? *And* wouldn't it be terrible for him to have to leave his school, his friends, his "baseball" team?

Three, his grandmother "probably shouldn't get too far away from the medical people who've been monitoring my condition." Verna had had an arrhythmic heartbeat from drinking too much coffee — once, five years before. She also had a medium-sized wart on the second finger of her left hand. In other words, she wasn't about to move into the house that Duncan had inherited.

"Suppose," said Mrs. Michalis, softly, "that Duncan wanted to go to a boarding school. Would that satisfy the . . . whatever you call them, the legalities?" She had her elbow on the table and she'd leaned her cheek against one finger, thoughtfully. Duncan had been pleased to see her back in her regular clothes again, a purple sweatshirt in this case, and a yellow scarf around her neck.

Verna's pencilled brows shot up. "I'm *sure* it would," she said, delightedly. "And if I understand the lawyers right, there's more than enough money for it."

Duncan was looking at both of them in horror. Boarding school? For him? They had to be kidding. He wasn't the type at all. Those kids were all rich, or stole from stores, or hadn't done their homework. A few of them were good ballplayers, of course, but they were mostly blacks, prepping for college and the NBA. Boarding school was *jail*, except that he'd be paying his good bucks for it — well, *Brian's* good bucks. How could Mrs. Michalis — who'd always been his buddy — suggest a thing like that?

"Well, then, if that's the case" — she still was mostly facing Verna — "why couldn't you let *me* be Duncan's boarding school? I would take responsibility — feed him, shelter him, even *supervise* him." She moved her head and hand real quickly, and he was pretty sure she'd winked at him. "And you could give us money every month for his expenses. He could stay in school, and keep on living here — or anyway next door, in my house. You *know* we get along," she said to Verna Williams.

"I wouldn't try to be your mother, Dunc." She'd turned and now was looking straight at him. "I'd just be me, your friend. Do you think you'd want to try it?"

Duncan looked across the table at his grandmother. He wasn't going to make his move too soon; he knew where all the power was in this game.

At first she tried to look reflective and judicious — properly concerned, the way a granny would be. But he could see (he thought) beyond, *behind*, that look. He thought it very doubtful that she'd ever be in a cell in the State Prison, listening to the warden say, "Well, Mrs. Williams, the governor has decided to grant you a full pardon; you won't be going to the electric chair at 12:01 A.M. tomorrow morning, after all." But if she ever *was*, she probably would look a lot like. . . .

Or was her face just mirroring his own?

13. HOME AWAY FROM HOME

For most of the first two weeks after it started, Duncan pretty much suckled on the novelty of living with — that's in the house of — Mrs. Dottie Michalis. The strangeness of the situation, and his feelings, captured his attention — froze him, more or less.

Grunfeld questioned him twice more, asking him if certain names meant anything to him, and where his brother went when he took "business trips," and how long he was gone. Duncan, knowing nothing useful, told him nothing useful. For that first fortnight, plainclothes cops put in a lot of hours watching Duncan and the house, but Duncan didn't know that, so he didn't care.

On the matter of the lawyer, he'd decided he

would wait a little while and see if there were any new developments; it still was vaguely possible (he told and *told* himself) there'd been some huge mistake — other people drove Trans-Ams and made themselves some dangerous enemies. And as far as Brian's message was concerned, there wasn't any tearing rush, he didn't think; anyway, it wasn't such an easy thing to do.

Besides, some nights, after he had gone to bed, he'd still start crying. Not quite the sort of act a guy would choose to travel with.

"I'd rather that you called me Dottie," she had said, the first night after Verna Williams left, the first night he had stayed inside her house. "But not as much as I want you to be comfortable. It doesn't really matter." And she'd looked away.

Duncan had smiled, and then had actually *said*, "I'll try to, Mrs. . . . *Dottie*," before (at least) he'd laughed, and blushed, thinking what an incredible goof he was, how *immature*.

He'd always thought she was a nice-looking lady, dark and . . . well, not fat, but obviously female. She wore tight, faded Levis and looked good in them, with sweatshirts and velour tops in outrageous colors, and a scarf around her neck. Her hair was done the way some Chinese ladies had their hair, very black and straight and short and shiny, with thick bangs almost to her eyebrows.

She turned out to be as casual and laid-back as a housemate as she'd been as a neighbor. It wasn't any wonder that his mother'd liked her so. They talked a lot, he and Dottie, more than he was used to. Partly, that was because they always sat down and ate together, almost every night. Apparently, she liked to cook, a lot more than his mother had. Before, he and Brian and his mother didn't necessarily do that. With them, a lot of times it was just a question of grabbing something to eat when you felt like it; there was always frozen stuff around. Once he got used to it, Duncan found that he enjoyed this new regime. Dottie didn't hesitate to bring up Brian and his mother, or to talk about her feelings. That made it possible for him to do the same. Gradually, the fact that they were dead moved downward from his mind and through the rest of him, and he accepted it. They were *really* dead, and always would be.

Dottie'd just assumed Brian had been dealing drugs all along, and so Duncan hadn't had to break the news to her. He was relieved by that. She'd heard Bri's standard speech about controls, and too much government, and private enterprise, and how society had its own self to blame for the rising crime rates (addict-crime was government-caused crime, he'd said). And how smart they were in England, drug-wise. And what a failure prohibitions always were. Duncan had thought of that speech as bullshit rationalizing, and apparently Dottie had, too.

She never asked him stuff about his schoolwork or the music that he listened to. That was a relief. His mother hadn't been too bad about that either; just from time to time she'd make a token show of parenting. What Dottie didn't do — at all — was push.

Both Terry's mother and Ben's mother had him over to their houses for supper, once a week both weeks, and when Dottie offered, he'd asked them both over to her place. He and Terry started to study together again, the way they'd always used to. Nobody said it, but everybody hoped to reconstruct a (so-called) normal life.

One night, when Dottie had some friends over, he and Terry decided to move their studying over next door, to his old house. For the time being, he'd put off the decision about what to do with it, if anything, and he'd been hanging out there, just from time to time, to see how that would feel. So far, he'd enjoyed it, but Terry hadn't been there for a while.

"Does this feel weird to you at all?" he asked her, after about an hour had gone by. They were sitting in the living room, where they'd usually studied before.

She shrugged. "I don't know. A little, maybe. It's okay, though; just different."

"I know," he said. "It sure is quiet, isn't it. No TV's and stuff. But even when Mom and Brian were out, it never seemed this quiet."

"Well," she said, "the phones aren't ringing all the time, for one thing. You remember how sometimes two different ones'd ring at once?"

"Yeah, that's right," he said, and nodded. They all had had to have their own phones, in that house. He looked down at his book again, and so did she.

"You know something else?" he said, a half an hour

later. It had taken twenty minutes' thought before he said that.

"No, what?" she said.

"We can do anything we want in here. I mean, now. Dottie'd never come in."

She looked at him very intently. He was staring at her with a small, strange smile on his face. Or maybe it wasn't a smile at all; you *could* say he looked more sad — or tense — than happy, really. She wasn't sure how he looked, except good. He looked good to her, as usual.

"Do you want to?" she said. He nodded. "And can we?"

That was a sort of code with them, meaning: Do you have any birth control?

He nodded once again. They went upstairs to his room.

"Let's take off all our clothes," he said. And all of a sudden he seemed to relax. He smiled again, this time a real enthusiastic, mischievous-looking smile, Terry thought. For all their having a private code and being very much into birth control, they were not experienced. They'd done a few things, but they'd never been in a place before where they could just begin by doing that, taking off all their clothes, to start with.

Terry didn't have any problems with her body, from the waist up, anyway; even the girls all said she had great tits. She thought her thighs and rear end were maybe a little heavier than they might be, but she loved Duncan a lot and he'd told her lots of times he liked her just the way she was. So she just stripped off her clothes real fast and didn't worry, tossing everything on the recliner. All her life she'd liked undressing, actually. That was either weird or natural, she thought, she wasn't sure which. She'd never talked it over with her mother.

When she was naked, she turned around toward him, smiling happily and bravely, conscious of the heartbeat in her chest; she was feeling very much the woman and very sure she was doing the right thing, for right then. He was just pushing down the skimpy briefs he wore. She raised a hand and popped her eyes and whistled; she just had to.

Then the phone rang in Brian's room, next door.

They'd stood there frozen, statues, Terry with her fingers to her mouth, a little chubby, maybe, but hard-chubby, smooth, her breasts set high, her nipples pink and pointed; Duncan, paler, tall, broad-shouldered, fat-free, clearly-muscled, not real hairy, very much aroused.

By the fourth ring, he'd gotten even paler. "I'd better answer it," he said.

He went to Brian's room, but didn't turn the light on. He felt his way along the edge of Brian's bed.

"Hello," he said.

"Who's this?" It was a voice he didn't recognize, a man.

"Who's *this*?" he said right back. Then decided he should add: "I'm Duncan, Brian's brother."

There was a pause. He shivered in the darkness. "Well, look," the voice began, "I think that he . . . that Brian . . . that your brother was meant to get, like, something sent to him today. Or it could be he was going to have to go and get it, I don't know. So, what I'm asking . . . what I want to know is, do you know, like, anything. . . ."

As the voice kept going, Duncan realized he didn't have a clue what he would say — *should* say — when it got to be his turn to speak again. He felt outstandingly naked. Probably this phone is tapped, he thought. And maybe this guy is a cop. He hung it up, by feel, and walked back to his room.

Terry had gotten into his bed and was lying there on her back, with the covers pulled up to her chin. She looked at him with an uncertain smile on her face, and waited. She didn't have the slightest idea what was going to happen.

Duncan sat down on the edge of the bed. She thought he looked as if he'd forgotten what they'd come up there for. He obviously wasn't as aware of her.

"I don't know," he said, and he shook his head. "I think we'd better go back next door. I'm sorry, Tare. I'm just a little freaked, I guess." He picked up his clothes off the floor and took them downstairs to put them on.

Terry got out of bed and dressed. While she did that, she decided that she wouldn't ask him anything about the call. She felt funny, on the edge of things.

On Wednesday of the third week that he'd been in Dottie Michalis' house, they were just finishing supper when he told her he was going to go, to leave.

At first, she'd cocked her head and simply raised an eyebrow, looking at her bowl, which held a little melted ice cream, mocha fudge.

"Go?" she said. Her voice didn't sound the same to him. "Go where? Go when?" Then she looked at him and her eyes filled up with tears; he was amazed.

"I thought this was working out pretty well," she said.

"Oh, it *is*." He heard the special pleading in his own voice, and she made a little quick motion with her hand, a motion of dismissal, a please-don't-lie-to-me.

"Really," he went on. "I promise you. It isn't this at all. It's . . . I don't know, everything else."

He leaned forward in his chair, with his arms circling his place mat and his empty bowl, and his hands clasped together. He was very clear in his head about what he wanted to do, what he was *going* to do, but he dreaded this part — having to say it all out loud. Not that he thought she'd try to stop him, necessarily. It was more that things always sounded different when you said them than when you felt or thought them.

"Well, you see." Duncan cleared his throat. "In the first place, it's — like — well, going to school. . . . Just lately, it's gotten completely unbearable, getting up every day — *you* know — and going over there and doing all that . . . stuff. I don't suppose it's any worse than it's ever been, but now — *I* don't know — I just have this feeling all the time, like I ought to be doing something else. You know?"

He raised his head so he could see her, check out her reaction. She was looking at him very steadily now, not crying and not smiling either. Just that steady, patient look of hers. Interested, you could say. Now she nodded slowly, up and down.

"Specifically," he said, "there's something else. Brian left me a note." He reached into his pocket for his wallet, got the little slip of paper out of it, and handed it across the table. He told her it had been in an envelope, and he told her what it had said on the outside of the envelope, in Brian's sort of language: "To be opened in the *absolutely* unlikely. . . ."

She read what he had given her, out loud. "Du-Du, check this out: fetish, swillys, boobytune." She pronounced the first word do-do, instead of duh-duh, Brian's way. She raised her eyebrows, looked at him. "I don't know what this means." She said that simply, flatly.

"Well," he said. He cleared his throat again. "The last two words are in this sort of code. I guess he did that just in case somebody else got ahold of the note. This way, it wouldn't make sense to anybody but me."

"Oh?" she said.

"Yes," he said. "It's a kind of a silly thing that Brian did." It made him mad to have said silly, like that; it sounded apologetic, disloyal. "Actually, it was sort of funny," he said. "And it worked. What he'd do was joke around with place names — like calling Westfield 'Wastepeel.' Get it? Like having nicknames for different places, funny ones. It was just a thing he did. Well, 'boobytune' is Burlington. And 'swillys' is a street, South Willard Street, in Burlington, Vermont."

"Wait." She chewed that over for a minute. She

was sharp. "I think I understand the code all right. But how do you know he didn't mean the Burlington right here in *this* state, or the one in Iowa, I think it is? Or that the street isn't Wilberforce or Williams? Or south of the Jeep dealer's? And how do you know that 'fetish' doesn't stand for *fetal rubbish*, or something?" She smiled, but sounded more on the impatient side, in the direction of pissed.

"I wasn't going to tell you," he said, "because I thought maybe the less you knew, the better for you. But I called Directory Assistance. On the phone? And there's a listing for someone or something named Fetish on a South Willard Street in Burlington, Vermont. 'A. Fetish,' like that. It has to be the one that Brian meant."

She took a deep breath. "I see," she said. "So you're going to drop out of school, and sneak out of town — I assume you're going to sneak — and go up there and 'check it out.' Is that it?"

He nodded. It was at this point that the whole thing got sort of hazy in his mind. He wasn't Simon & Simon, or Magnum P.I. What did he know about checking anything out? He hoped she wouldn't ask.

"The thing is," he said, "I don't know anything about the stuff that Bri was doing — just that he was doing it. And so there's nothing I can tell the cops, or anyone. But everybody seems to think I can, that I know a lot of details. I feel like such a total pigeon, hanging out down here. I need to *do* something," he said, "even if it's just get out of the way for a while." He decided he wouldn't say anything about how he'd come to realize that if *he* was in any danger, he was putting her in danger, too, just by staying — being — in her house. Or how even more terrified he was for Terry. Look what happened to his mother. He decided not to use such words as *freaked*, or *paranoid*, either. "Do you think I'm really being crazy?"

"Yes," she said. "I do. I think you're out of your mind. I *liked* Brian, you know that; I liked him a lot. But the guy was . . . well, a little off the wall, let's face it. Who knows what you might find up there? I don't mean to be flip, but for all you know this Fetish is a tombstone carver, or something. Did you call the number up there?"

Duncan shook his head. "I don't want to," he said. "I want to go. I've thought about it lots. I guess you can try to stop me, or tell the police where I am, but I hope you don't. I'm asking you not to, Dottie."

She looked at him and smiled again, but this time she looked sad. "I won't try to stop you," she said. "And I won't tell the cops where you are. The only thing I'll ask you to do is stay in touch with me, somehow. I'm sure there must be a way, even if this phone is tapped."

And so there was: They figured one out. Monday through Friday, Dottie took her lunch to work and ate it outside on a park bench that was near a public phone booth. She would get the number of that phone, and he could take it with him, call her any weekday that it wasn't raining, any time from quarter-past to half-past twelve. She'd always be there, then. Unless, of course, it happened to be raining.

"Of course I'll call you," Duncan said. "I want to." He needed to say something more. "I really love you,

Dottie. And not just because you took me in, and all. I think you're the nicest person that I've ever met. And don't worry. Please. I've got a feeling this is one of Brian's really *good* ideas, I really do." He reached out and put a hand on hers, and squeezed it.

Then, of course, she *did* cry — standing up to do so and starting to walk around the table toward him. And he stood up and hugged her, feeling lots of different feelings, including some he couldn't quite believe.

60

14. DISGUISES

Duncan bought the glasses at the enormous Woolworth's downtown, right when all the offices were letting out and the place was mobbed. They had big black plastic frames and the lenses were just plain glass. He couldn't get over how different they made him look.

Dottie gave him the haircut, after he'd taken a comb and parted his hair on the other side. She did a nice, neat job, and also quick, and right afterwards they drove down to the Humane Society. That didn't take long, either. They walked in and he saw this one dog stretched out on his side. And the dog opened one eye, just craning his neck a little, and when he saw it was Duncan, he jumped right up, mouth open, eyes smiling, tail a-wag. Like he'd been waiting patiently for just that perfect person to arrive: the one he was *meant* to have, and take good care of, always. He looked like a cross between a Lab and a shepherd, but a compact model, maybe two thirds the size of each. His ears were pointed, but they flopped; his coat was smooth and mostly brown, with a little black up on one shoulder. He had big feet, like Duncan.

Once he was sure Dottie knew which one, Duncan went outside again and let her do the lying to the lady. She'd stuffed all her hair under a beret and put on a ton of makeup. When she came out with the dog, he looked around, saw Duncan, and ran and jumped right up in front of him, as high as his chest, where Duncan caught him and let him lick his face. That one jump earned him his name, The Skywalker, or Sky for short. He knew that name by morning, and he already knew when to "Sit."

What Duncan figured was: If he waited for the first sunny, dry day, it'd take a pretty hard-hearted driver to pass up a tall, studious-looking, short-haired, neatly dressed boy with a happy, clean, obedient puppy dog, on a leash, with a red bandana on.

And it'd take a miracle for *anyone* to find their trail.

15. LETTER

Dear Terry,

This is the hardest letter I've ever had to write in my life, by far. Not that I've written all that many!

Here's the story: I'm going away for a little while. I don't know exactly when I'll be coming back, but it shouldn't be too long. It kind of depends.

The thing is, I just can't stand going to school every day and acting like I'm leading a "normal" life, when nothing feels the same any more. Wait. I don't mean us — *that* feels the same. I still love you, the way I always have, but the rest of my life doesn't seem the same at all. Can you possibly understand what I mean? I'm *sure* you can. Sometimes you understand me better than I do!

Anyway. Before, a lot of what was going on — at school and stuff — seemed stupid and messed up, but I'd gotten kind of used to it, I guess. But what happened to Mom and Brian was sort of like the last straw, the one "that broke the camel's back," as they say. You've seen the way I've been acting. I just can't seem to handle it. What gets me is that if the cops have any leads at all, they sure aren't admitting it to me; the only thing they keep on saying is that I should keep my eyes open and watch my step. But what am I meant to look for? It's all crazy. I feel like I'm in a bad dream, or an actor in a play where everyone knows their lines and the plot, except me.

I know what you might be thinking: Probably the world stinks just as much wherever a person goes. And that's probably right. Never having been much of anywhere, I couldn't say for sure. It seems like people are so rotten nowadays that all they can think of is getting theirs and too bad for whoever's in the way. It's depressing (to put it mildly!).

What I'm hoping, though, is that if I have a total change for a while, I'll feel different than I do now — more like a kid who's got college and a good life to look forward to. That's the way I want to feel, I really do — as if they're things to look forward to again. To be honest with you, the way I feel right now I wouldn't care if I never picked up a basketball again. Maybe a "vacation" can help me the way it's meant to help older people.

One last thing (whew!). You've been the greatest during all of this, just the way you always are. I'll be in touch as soon as I can be. Just — PLEASE — don't worry and try to understand what I'm feeling. Take it easy, Tare.

All my love,
Duncan

P.S. Please tell Ben as much of this as you want to and thank him for being great, too.

P.P.S. Please don't say *anything* to *anyone else*, cops included. As a matter of fact, it'd be *much better* if you'd burn this letter when you're through reading it. Or flush it down the toilet so your mother won't smell something burning and get all . . . *you* know.

16. SWILLYS

Because Duncan Banigan had been born and raised in one of the flatter sections of New Jersey, he'd never had the chance to notice that when a town is built on the side of a slope, the richer people live (where else?) at the top and the poorer people at the bottom. That way, the richer people get the nice views, as well as the opportunity to look down their noses on a regular basis, while the poorer people are thankfully relieved of the burden of having to walk up that goldurn hill every time they want to go home.

Burlington, Vermont, is built on the shores of Lake Champlain, which is not only one hundred twenty-five miles long, running north and south, and the western border of lots of Vermont, but also flows calmly across the Canadian border and into southern Quebec. A lot of Burlington is lake shore flat, but inland just a little ways the ground begins to tilt, and pretty soon you start to see some big old houses. The no-frills name for this attractive part of town is the Hill Section. The University is at the very top of it, and Champlain College just a step below. South Willard Street's between the two of them, in places, and that's where Duncan and his new best friend were walking back and forth when they attracted Caitlin Fetish.

They had two reasons for this walking-back-and-forth routine: One of them (that's either Duncan or the dog) was trying to think, a bit uncertain, up a tree, you might say; the other one, he just enjoyed the walking, after eight full hours in — let's see — five different cars. Which one was which? It doesn't really matter, does it? Dogs and guys are pretty interchangeable, at times.

Duncan, frankly, was surprised at what they'd found at the address beside the name "A. Fetish" in the phone book. He'd expected . . . well, an ordinary house, perhaps with nice white clapboards on the sides, like lots of others. Or maybe an apartment building, small and brick, with eight electric meters counting money on the side of it. Instead, it was a mansion — rambling, huge, four stories high — made of brick and red stone, with a vast slate roof on lots of different levels, and a curving drive, and a carriage house out back, no less. Beside the massive wooden door (complete with heavy, round brass knocker) there was a plaque of weathered bronze. Its dark, raised letters stated this: The Friends of Nukismetic Humanism.

College-ready-or-not, Duncan did not know, and could not figure out for sure, what Nukismetic Humanism was. Would he and Sky be "friends" of it, or not? In the shadowed, S.A.T.-ish section of his mind, there weren't any certainties on *human*ism, but there was the information that *de*ism was a system of thought that didn't believe much in God, or any other deities. So maybe humanism didn't believe much in people? He could buy that. But where did nukismetic fit in? Didn't that have something to do with coin-collecting? He simply wasn't sure.

In the half hour or so that they'd been walking back and forth, he'd seen a number of people go into and come out of the building, and they had not been frightening. They looked to be of college age or older, men and women both, all dressed about the same in running shoes and jeans and turtlenecks, checked shirts, down vests, and sixty-forties. Almost half the men, he guessed, had beards and most of them did quite a bit of smiling, waving, using words like *Ciao*. But still, for all of that, he hadn't gotten up the nerve to go and knock and ask for Mister Fetish (or should he mumble "Mizz," and cough, in case?). And if that very person answered, what would he say to him or her? Back home, he'd thought a simple "Hi, I'm Duncan Banigan" would do, with maybe "Brian's brother" tacked to it. Now, that seemed . . . well, *unstrategic*, you could say — or even dangerous.

They had paused in their walking back and forth

and were standing (and sitting) directly in front of the place. Duncan was scratching his head and thinking that he'd come two hundred and fifty miles to find this house but now couldn't seem to take the last thirty steps to enter it when a female voice behind him said:

"You *can't* be as lost as you look. Can you?"

He turned and faced the voice. Seeing her, his first thought was I'll bet she's played some ball; his second was My God, she's gorgeous. His third one: First things first, right, Banigan? You're weird.

Caitlin Fetish was, in fact, a hair over six feet tall in her Dunham Duraflex boots. She was also slender and green-eyed and had very long, very straight, light brown hair, almost to her waist. When Duncan paid attention to the length of it, he figured that she wasn't active as a player *now*, most likely; hair that long would be a pain, unless she put it up like dancers did — and would that stay? He also saw that she was older, in her twenties he would guess. She had fair skin and wide cheekbones and her green eyes were very slightly slanted and her chin was very slightly pointed; she looked like a slender, long-haired, green-eyed wolf. Sky must have thought she looked like kinfolks, too; he rubbed against her leg while making *very* friendly sounds. Almost too friendly, for kinfolks.

"Well — um, ah, yeah. I guess we are at that. Lost," said Duncan, answering at last. But by then she'd done a deep knee bend and was down there patting Sky, both hands on his ears and almost (pointed) nose to nose.

"Oh, is he ever *beautiful!*" she said. "What's his name? I love him."

"Sky," he said. "For short. The Skywalker. He has a forty-two inch vertical leap," he said, extemporizing.

She turned her head, looked up at him. "You're kidding," she suggested, and he smiled and shrugged and hoped he looked like fun.

"I bet you're up here to look at the University," she said. "The season's just beginning now. High school juniors by the hundreds, checking out the good old U." She stood and peered at him more closely. "I'm not insulting you, I hope. Maybe you're accepted at fair Harvard for the fall, already. But what with that" — she nudged the pack on Duncan's back — "and him" — she pointed down at Sky, who wagged delightedly and would have pointed back, if he were able — "you've got a certain look about you. A person on a little spring adventure — expedition — up at UVM, with a stop at Middlebury on the way back down. Don't get me wrong. I mean it as a compliment," she said, and laughed. It was a cheerful, friendly, nonjudgmental sort of sound, thought Duncan.

"Well, not exactly." Duncan started badly. His mind was floundering; she'd caught him unprepared. What *was* he doing there? "But *sort* of," he went on. "That is, I *am* real interested in coming here, I think. And — uh — this is our spring vacation, back at school. So what I'm going to do is *live* up here awhile, I think, and take an *in-depth* look at college, you might say, and. . . ." Out of all that blah-blah-blah came

Inspiration, pure and crisp and oh-so-very welcome:
". . . and maybe get permission from my school *to do
my Junior Project* here." This Junior Project jazz was
something that he'd heard about from Benny's dopey
older brother Tim, who'd been shipped away to prep
— far out in Colorado. And suddenly it was as if he'd
stolen an inbounds pass at midcourt, with clear sail-
ing to the hoop.

The girl picked up her eyebrows.

"What *that* is" — he dribbled wildly on — "is a
really innovative program. For juniors in the A.P.
track. It's called Urban-Suburban Survival, and what
you're meant to do is go somewhere with only fifty
bucks and make it for two months on that. Find a job,
and get a place to live, and keep a journal all the time
on the experience: what happens, what you learn,
your different feelings, and all that. The whole *concept*" — Duncan crossed the foul line and took off,
soaring through the air, the ball above his head — "is
called Experiential Education." Slamma-Jamma-
Dunkenstein!

"Huh," she said and made a mouth — impressed, it
looked like. "So what you're looking for is just a place
to stay, a job, and some . . . experiences, right?" She
flicked up fingers one through three while saying that
— in rather a sarcastic tone, thought Duncan. But
then she grinned.

"Well, this may be your lucky day," she said. "The
place you see before you here might possibly supply
all three. We'll have to ask my father. He's in charge,
as much as anybody is; the whole thing's his idea.
And here's a guarantee." She laughed aloud again.

"'Live here and you will have experiences. You know what Nukismetic Humanism is? Of course you don't, why should you? Don't let me scare you — nothing kinky, or all that. *I* think it's crazy, but . . . you'll see. I'm just his daughter so I live here. And of course I love the guy. You want to check it out?" He gulped and nodded.

She stuck out a long, lean, smooth, strong hand. "Okay. I'll take you in and introduce you. I'm Caitlin Fetish. If you ever call my Kitty, I will bite your ear-lobes off."

With which she tossed her hair and laughed some more and headed down the curving drive, with Sky right after her.

Duncan followed, too. He knew he was feeling different than he'd felt in three weeks. What he didn't know — or at least think about, right then — was *how*, *to what extent*, or *why*.

17. MORE IS BETTER (BABY)

"I'll tell you this much," Police Chief Boris "Babe" DeBoardman said to Sergeant Rodney Hamill, Bomb Squad (State Police). But before he did, he blew into the cardboard cup of coffee (light) he'd wrapped his big right hand around. "The guy was not the hippie type. More what folks would call old-fashioned, even, for a guy that age. The suit; still living with his mom; an usher down at St. Teresa's. Sorta kid you wouldn't mind your daughter takes an interest in. Once he got blown up, this Grunfeld here in my department comes down with twenty-twenty hindsight like you can't believe: He knew the guy was into *something*, all along. Yeah, sure, Grunter; you bet. Drugs, most likely, that's his theory now. Me, I just don't know. But still" — the chief gave one huge shoulder-shrug — "you still got questions on the message board." He put his coffee down and raised his hand, then moved it left to right. "Where'd he get his money from? Why'd he get blown up? By who? And now the latest: What's become of not-so-little brother Duncan?"

"So the *brother's* missing now," said Sergeant Hamill. He looked at Trooper Giambelluca as he said that, and gave a little nod, the corners of his mouth turned down. It was his "what did I just tell you?" face, and Trooper G. had seen a lot of it the past three weeks. It almost always made no sense to him, but he was smart enough to nod right back at it and sometimes wink (which clearly meant, "You called it, chief.")

"Yes," said the police chief. "For the past three days. The lady he was living with, the neighbor, said he left for school the same as usual. He never got there; we know that. Grunter thinks he skipped to save his neck, before they got to him. Or possibly to dig for buried treasure, if you get my meaning. Me, I doubt that very much. The kid was All-State basketball, first team. That's *including* prep and public. Plus he's Catholic League Player of the Year. And Student Honor Society, class officer, busboy at McDonald's sometimes. Frankly, Rod, I'm worried," said Boris "Babe" DeBoardman. But he didn't *look* worried. He smiled at Sergeant Hamill. "What we're hoping is you're going to give us dopes a place to start from, anyway. So, how about it, Sherlock — what did all

that mess of blowup tell the brain-boys this time?"
And he chuckled at his very well-put flattery. The
guy had taken three full weeks; he'd *better* have a lot to
flatter.

Sergeant Hamill almost always loved that moment
dearly, when they asked him what his findings were.
He could then sit back and string it out, happy in the
spotlight: what was used, and where it might have
been procured, and how it was installed, with what
degree of expertise, and if the guy was tall or short,
black or white, briefs or boxers on, and blond, bru-
nette, or redhead. And he'd go along with "genius" at
the end, if they insisted.

But this time here was the exception.

"Babe, I got bad news," he said. "This is the one
case in a million. Frankly, I've never seen a job
botched up like this before, thank God. What happened is these sons-a-bitchin' amateurs did it ass-
hole-deep in four leaf clovers, shitcha not. They used
so much and put it in so screwy that when it went,
well, everything went with it. The kid" — he jerked a
thumb toward Giambelluca — "and me have put that
Trans-Am through a strainer, and there's absolutely
nothing there. We haven't got a thing for you. The
only thing we learned for sure is this: The guys
that blew up Banigan and his old lady were totally
incompetent."

Trooper Giambelluca nodded solemnly, agreeing
with his chief. But also with himself. Of course he
wouldn't say it right out loud, but: More *was* better,
baby — just as he had always known it was. Tell *him*
America ain't beautiful. . . .

18. ANNOYANCE PHONE CALL

He always said, "I want please, to speak with Mister Duncan Banigan." Not "Hello," or "May I?" ever.

Dottie always said, "I'm sorry, he's not here." And, "If you'll give me your name and number, I'll have him call when he comes in."

At least she "always" said that for the first five times he called.

And he would answer back. "No, thank you. Better I will call back later." His voice was not a kid's, and didn't sound official, like a cop's voice would. Cops did not have accents, Dottie told herself.

After five, she started hanging up on him. She got to know his "I," and didn't have to wait for "want."

19. NU-HU

Caitlin Fetish hadn't asked his name, but when they'd barely gotten in the door, he'd met two guys with smiles and beards who greeted him as cordially as college scouts and bellowed, on the one hand, "Roger!" (short, well-trimmed, but graying) and "Justin!" with a firm grip, too (curly-brown and Santa-Claus-ish, with the mustache shaved).

So naturally he'd smiled right back at them and yodeled "Duncan," just as cheerfully, and she had learned his name from that and used it introducing him to others they ran into on the stairs, and to her father on the second floor. "The family" was quartered there, spread out over six or seven rooms at least, by Duncan's guess, while "the residents" were doubled — sometimes tripled — up, above them on the third and fourth. A lot of "Friends" lived elsewhere, on their own.

"Daddy, this is Duncan," she had said.

"Abraham Fetish," her father volunteered to him. He looked happy about it, even though he had no facial hair and not an awful lot on top. His face was large and full, and also very pink and clean. The Fetishes — there didn't seem to be a Mrs./mom — appeared to be the only people there who mentioned their last name.

Now, two meals, a good night's sleep, and many fascinating conversations later, Duncan was sitting on one of the "house" (meaning not privately owned) meditation cushions, looking up at that same Fetish, Abraham. Because, both in and out of season, Duncan did his stretching exercises, his legs were properly entwined in a modest, neat half-lotus. Sky already had transcended everything; he lay at Duncan's side, conked out.

"The state we seek, and will attain, is not a blank," said Fetish. His voice was rolling, resonant; it slowly sounded every word it touched, from start to finish, the way a hand will pat a cat. "A blank is emp-ty, vul-ner-able, weak. We must be *for*-ti-fied, pro*tec*-ted." He bent his arm and raised the pointer finger, and his voice. " 'He shall be *peace*-ful in a ring of fire, like the lover on his bed of water, even as the cool-ness of his flame rejects the cat-as-troaf.' Emil 4, 15."

Abraham Fetish was a huge man, "as big as olden doors" (as Mister Carlo liked to say). For this beginners' class in Nukismetic Humanism's brand of (useful) meditation, he had chosen to wear a floor-length, unisex white lounging robe, with purple trim (an XXLarge), the exact same robe that sold for nineteen dollars and ninety-five cents at the store on Shelburne Road, and ditto, postpaid, through the mails. It had the letters NU-HU on the high left breast, something like a monogram.

Duncan already knew, of course that NU-HU was the trademark name of the line of health products — oil, shampoos, and soaps, as well as foods and dietary supplements, not to mention proper clothes to wear while feeling healthy — produced and marketed by the Nukismetic Humanists. NU-HU also was, as Caitlin Fetish had envisioned, his employer, starting later on that day.

In the seventeen hours that Duncan had been in the house on South Willard Street — not counting the hour's run he'd taken with Sky, earlier that same morning — he had gotten not only a job and a third floor room (complete with roommate), and a cushion in a meditation class, but also lots of information, some of it amazing.

After supper, the first night, he and Sky had strolled around the first floor of the house, watched a little tube, and played (and also watched) a game of Ping-Pong; everyone was very, very friendly. After that, they went upstairs, with early bedtime on their minds. His roommate, Christopher, was in the room, though, lying on his waterbed and reading; he stopped when they came in and smiled a greeting.

And that's when Duncan learned what Nukismetic Humanism *was*. He got Chris started on the explanation by asking him straight out and suddenly if all the Friends were coin collectors. Christopher looked blank at first, so Duncan said, "The *nukismetic* part. Isn't that like coin-collecting, for a hobby?"

Christopher then smiled, a vague and gentle one, and switched his eyes off to one side, as if he feared a joke was sneaking up on him, perhaps.

"That, I think, is *numismatics*," he said softly. At five foot six, and slight, he always tiptoed up to people Duncan's size, at least until he got to know them better.

Christopher was also beardless, having no more choice in the matter than Duncan did. But he proudly had produced, above an overbite, a sparse and silky mustache, as well as long, straight, shiny light brown hair that covered up his ears and hit his shoulders on each side, except when he was working at the store and used a rubber band on it, to keep it out of people's cheese or honey. Christopher was seventeen and formerly had lived near Three Mile Island, Pennsylvania; he'd never liked the place, it had a certain atmosphere, he said — and showed his top front teeth, and licked his lips. Apparently, he'd first heard about Nukismetic Humanism on an all-night radio talk show. Some guy had called up pissed because his kid had taken up with it instead of going in with *him*, selling "this dynamite line of trash compacters," door to door. The guy had described what NKH was all about and then had kept on saying to the host, "Well, isn't that just absolute and total *bullbleep*?

"He actually said 'bullbleep' on the radio," said Christopher, laughing now, and shaking his head. "I thought that was so funny. But he was a good salesman, all right. He sold me without even trying to. Of course he didn't have to, in a way.

"I think that most intelligent people" — he nodded at Duncan — "are ready for NKH *long* before they even hear of it. I know I was. For one thing, you've got to be pretty obtuse not to see how phenomenally messed up the whole world is, what with the Russian leaders lying to their people and whoever else'll listen to them, and the American leaders doing the exact same thing, almost. It's gotten to the point where you can't believe anyone, totally. That's pathetic, *I* think. My parents used to vote straight Democrat, but not any more; now, half the time they like what the Republican is saying — or think that both the candidates are full of it. Even the scientists don't seem to know what's going on nowadays — either that or they're lying just as much as the rest of them. One group says that yes, there can be nice clean strategic weapons, even if they're nuclear. To hear *them* talk, this neutron bomb is sort of like the opposite of Memorex — the recording tape? It kills the Russians in the tank, but doesn't even *chip* the stemware." He laughed again and tossed his hair back.

"Then, on the other hand," he continued, "you get the ones like Schell or Helen Caldicott telling you there's no such thing as 'limited,' when it comes to nuclear war. And if you can find any normal genes after one, they'll be either blue or cockroach's." Christopher giggled. "So who's a person meant to believe?"

Christopher didn't wait for an answer. "Well, the one thing that seemed pretty obvious to *me*," he said, "was that what with all the lying and confusion going on, *plus* all the building up of warheads, missiles, all that junk, there probably would *have* to be a war, and sometime soon. But that it probably wouldn't be either as clean and limited as some of the Pentagon people were saying, or as catastrophic as the Caldicotts said. It'd be somewhere in between, is what I thought — limited in some places, you could say, and maybe totally destructive in others, depending.

"Okay." Christopher tucked one thin leg up on his bed, and sat on it. "So that was what I already thought about war, before I ever heard of NKH. But at the same time I'd also done a lot of worrying about world population. The kids on Three Mile Island all thought I was crazy, but anyone with half an ounce of brains can see we've got a problem. It's not just that there's too many people, it's what happens to them when they're overcrowded. You heard about the rat experiments? How when researchers overcrowded them — this bunch of rats — their families broke up, and self-respecting peaceful rats turned into rapists, robbers, and murderers? It's a fact. And now we've got — what is it? — six hundred million Chinese? Or is it a billion already? Can you imagine that many rapists and murderers running around? I mean, not that the Chinese ever would, but . . . *you* know. *Forget* it. Even here in Burlington — you'll see — there isn't any place at all to park downtown, or in the malls on Saturdays.

"But what I hadn't done, don't ask me why," he said, "was put the two things together: the nuclear war problem and the population problem. I didn't see — until the Nukismetic Humanists explained it, or actually this nutty salesman did — that two huge wrongs might sort of make a right. Add nuclear war to an overcrowded and immoral planet, and you get the same effect as you do when you thin out a row of lettuce in the garden, maybe. The fewer plants grow strong and healthy, having space to be themselves! What the people here believe is that nuclear technology was *fated* — that's the 'kismet' part, means 'fate' in Arabic or something — to serve mankind. To save us from ourselves and all the rest of our technology. So Nukismetic Humanism is just what its name suggests: the belief in a fated nuclear encounter — between ourselves and the Russians, presumably — for the eventual benefit of humanity."

Duncan started to speak, but before he could, Christopher leaned way forward and tapped him on the knee.

"I know," he said. "It's gross to think about. But I think it's even more gross to think about your grand-children slowly starving to death or being raped and murdered. I'm not going to sit here and tell you the war I'm talking about won't be hell. Of course it will be. But let me tell you something else, so you'll know how much I believe in what I'm saying. I've always felt. . . *believed* — I've *humanistically* believed — that *no* one (my father would be a perfect example of the *opposite* of this) should ask *any*body to do something he's not willing to do himself. Not push the button, or save the child, or slaughter the hog, or get a beer from the refrigerator. So I can tell you in absolute honesty that although I'm probably *not* going to be one of the ones who's going to have to die so's to make the planet livable again, if I had to I would. And perfectly happily." He bobbed his head up and down quickly. "That may be hard to believe, but it's the truth."

Duncan only nodded, rose, and went into the bathroom. When he'd brushed his teeth and pissed, he'd come back in and gone to bed. That was pretty typical of him. He liked to think an idea through before he started shooting off his mouth. He'd never been a pop-off. So what he did that night was smile at Christopher and say good-night to him — just so he'd know he wasn't mad or anything — and then lie down and close his eyes. Christopher was okay — a little different, but okay. They'd get along, no problem. Christopher was friendly.

Nukismetic Humanism, though, seemed slightly odd and not so friendly. Semiplausible on the surface, maybe, but not . . . acceptable, not good. He'd learned a word in school that year, *sophistry*: "the art of making bullshit smell like a begonia," as earthy Brother Alphonse had put it. Nukismetic Humanism looked like that, to him. And in spite of what Christopher had said about being happy to die, it was pretty obvious that the Friends were planning to survive the war they thought was coming. He wondered how they thought they'd manage that. He wondered if maybe they thought that the Russian leaders and the American leaders had worked out a deal on who drops bombs where, so that people on the inside (like the Russian and American leaders and their families and friends — and *Friends*?) could arrange to be somewhere else.

Wow (thought Duncan), that'd mean that the two countries had worked out some sort of *population* limitation pact, instead of the arms limitation treaty everyone thought they were negotiating. Was that conceivable? Was it remotely possible that Abraham Fetish had stumbled onto something that nobody else knew, some absolutely top-secret stuff about international agreements and the latest technology on ways to limit the effects of nuclear fallout? He wondered if scientists, given enough time and money, could do *anything* imaginable. Which politicians would then take advantage of, of course.

What he didn't have to wonder any more, though, was why Brian had sent him to this place. Brian had known how bad he'd been feeling for the last half year or so, how bummed out he'd been by noticing the way that nothing (almost) worked the way it should. How it seemed to be a fact that not just weather forecasts and schools but most — two thirds, at least — of all the dentists, doughnuts, drivers, delis, and (luckily) defensive players that people had to deal with simply weren't any *good*.

So, busy as he was, Bri had looked around and found this place for Duncan. Maybe he had even had a hunch — a psychic flash — that he might die, and what would happen to his little brother then? If the Nukismetic Humanists were right (so Bri would have it figured), Duncan might survive the war with them, and then enjoy their smaller post-war world (in terms of numbers), a world that they maintained would work a whole lot better, out from under all that over-crowding pressure.

What a sweetheart Brian was (Duncan thought, before he fell asleep); what a world where guys like him got killed!

Of course, in the clear light of morning he remembered that lots of things that Brian raved about ("amazing!" and "the greatest!" or "a breakthrough!") turned out to be a little . . . disappointing. Seven out of ten, he'd say. At least.

20. AURAS

"All right, now. Time, please, everyone." Fetish's deep voice was loud and rich in chest tones — as it always was — but it was also more decisive, business-like, official. A pass-your-blue-book-to-the-person-on-your-right type voice.

Duncan opened first one eye and then the other; if anyone was watching him, perhaps they'd think that he'd been doing meditation (as he should have been) and not just sitting there waist deep — or "pecker high," as Benny liked to say — in fantasies and wonders. It seemed to him that maybe people here (like Fetish, Abraham) *did* know some things that no one else had gotten onto yet.

"A lot of you are doing well," said Fetish. "I see

some splendid change, in color *and* intensity. You're starting to develop greens and even turquoise, here and there. Mona! Great — terrific! Yours had flickers of an aqua that's just *perfect*. Maximum. Really quite remarkable." A curly haired young woman in the back first blushed, then squirmed with pleasure on her cushion, which was purple with a unicorn embroidered on the top of it. She had on a very tight white jump suit that made her perfect lotus all the more . . . remarkable. Duncan had noticed her before the meditating started; he thought she looked more like the kind of girl you'd see at a car race, like the Daytona 500, or a hang-gliding competition. And here she was a crack beginning meditator, more of a *spiritual* sort of person. It just goes to show, he thought: Judgments should be come to slowly — very, very slowly.

"Remember this, I beg of you," said Fetish. "A person's aura isn't just her spirit-skin, or his: another epidermal layer, outside and touching on the one we wash, and sometimes paint or dress so lovingly. It *can* be made to stand away from one, like the halo in a medieval masterpiece. And so I want you to *push out* against your aura, even as you cool the colors down. That distance is defensively important." He raised a reasonable palm. "No, it isn't easy, but it can be done: cool and push, together. Thinking all the time in terms of nice pale blue, or greenish blue, perhaps six inches off the body, all the way around. Right now, a lot of you would — hah! — have trouble with a dental X ray, but don't worry, you can get it if you practice hard enough. And when you do — I promise you —

you'll then be radiation-safe at fifty miles from blast. And none of us should ever have to be *that* close, no way." Fetish smiled and folded his large hands above the NU-HU on his front.

Duncan hadn't heard much aura talk before — just that everybody had one. According to some people, anyway. The thing went all around the body (if you thought it went at all) and sometimes changed its color, depending on your mood. He'd never heard that anyone believed an aura could be used the way that Fetish said it could be: defensively, against radiation. According to him, it was at least the equal of a lead shield, or a good three feet of topsoil. And a hell of a lot handier. It seemed a little wild, this thought, until you stopped to consider stuff like those guys over in India, or that general region, who actually did walk on top of red-hot coals with feet no more callused than his own. That had actually been documented on TV. Who was to say they weren't protected by their auras?

Because it was almost a reflex for a guy who played School as well as he did, Duncan put his hand up. An interested question never hurt. Fetish nodded at him, smiling.

"Sir," said Duncan, "I'm wondering about my dog. I don't suppose it's possible to teach him meditation, is it? Assuming dogs have auras, which" — he gave the am-I-being-foolish? laugh the nuns had always seemed to like, in grade school — "I, of course, can't tell yet."

Fetish chuckled, a paternal, friend of animals. "Well, when you can, you'll see that yes, they do," he said. "And seeing them can be a help, at times. As, for example, when you meet a strange Doberman in a dark alley. But — your question. The problem is — would be — to train the animal to change, and then *maintain* a certain color for a certain time." Fetish shrugged. "I doubt it can be done. But what you *can* do, I believe, is this: You can make space inside your own — elasticize it, as it were. Or loosen it, you might say. Sufficiently to pull a dog inside of it in an emergency, or even — should the need arise — a *daughter*. Hah!" cried Fetish, happily. Others laughed along with him. "Everybody knows," he said to Duncan, in a kindly way, "my daughter is . . . *unorthodox*." He winked. "A scoffer. We'll practice — just the two of us, all right? — it could be quite a breakthrough." He cleared his throat; up went that finger, once again. " 'To him who pays the price with a benignant heart, a passionate vitality, and an unfettered mind, shall all the mysteries expose themselves,'" he preached. "Panjandrum 43, 15."

Duncan smiled and mouthed a thank you, as the class broke up. He patted Sky and wondered what his aura-color was, right then. A sort of sleepy tan, perhaps. He wondered who Panjandrum was; it sounded like a word he'd read in Barron's Guide. It couldn't be from Gilbert and Sullivan, could it? Would a humanist have saints?

In any case, their next appointment of the day was lunch, and after that they'd wait for Caitlin Fetish, who'd said she'd take them to the store that afternoon, and show them what the job involved. Apparently, she didn't scoff at NU-HU products. In fact, she'd told him she put in a lot of hours on the business end of Nukismetic Humanism. It got a little much sometimes, she said, what with all the hours that she had to spend at school — but still, she managed.

Duncan wasn't too surprised to hear that she did that — all that. He thought she was about the most . . . capable-looking girl he'd ever seen. During meditation practice, he'd imagined how she must have looked in a basketball uniform, assuming that she'd played. He'd imagined her with shorter hair, and fairly snug-fitting shorts, with slits on the sides, and a silky sleeveless top and, as a matter of absolute but unlikely fact, no bra. He also imagined that the ring she'd been wearing the day before was her mother's old engagement ring that her father had asked her to wear after her mom had died. Maybe in an accident — something like that.

21. T-BIRD

Caitlin Fetish drove a 1957 Ford T-bird, white, with a black cloth top. Her father Abraham had bought it new, the year it was made, because he thought it was the sexiest-looking car he'd ever seen. And the next year, sure enough, his daughter Caitlin was born, so he put the car up on blocks in a garage he'd rented in the country and didn't take it down until 1979, when he gave it to Caitlin on her twenty-first birthday.

Well, she thought it was the sexiest car she'd ever seen, too, but a lot of things had changed in twenty-two years, some for the better. After graduation from college and a year in the WBL (yes, she'd been a player, sure enough), she applied to and was accepted in the doctoral program in clinical psychology at UVM, still childless. Abraham Fetish had a nagging sense of having been outwitted. He'd wanted a grandchild, not a doctor, and now with Caitlin seemingly engaged to Lisle Hardaway, soon-to-be-MD, he might have two — not twins, but doctors.

"Talk about reverse psychology," he'd said to Mister Carlo, once. Mister Carlo laughed although, as usual, he wasn't sure he got it.

When, after lunch (he ate some things he'd never heard of in his life, before) Duncan saw that T-bird, parked, top-down, with Caitlin waiting in the driver's seat, the stereo alive and kickin', he also thought that it was the sexiest car he'd ever seen. He tried to imagine the sound that Ben might have made, in his shoes. He decided there would not have been a sound. Benny's circuits couldn't have absorbed that overload; he would have been unconscious on the sidewalk, with little wisps of smoke escaping from his body, here and there.

Sky loved the T-bird, too. Because it had a bench seat, of a sort, there was a place a dog could sit, between the two of them. Whenever Caitlin turned a corner, Sky would lean against a shoulder — his or hers, depending. Then he'd get his balance and sit straight again. He liked the motion and the top-down smell and being flanked by two real fans of his. He didn't think the car was all that sexy, though. As a dog, he didn't mix up sex and transportation.

"So. How you doing so far?" Caitlin said to Duncan, as they started out. "Experientially, I mean." She took a peek at him and laughed, but once again he heard her laugh as friendly, sort of like a teammate's laugh, rather than a mock.

"Pretty good," he said. "I got the whole philosophy from Christopher last night. My roommate, Christopher? Real long hair, buck teeth, a little mustache?" She nodded. "Then, this morning I had meditation class and learned about our auras and their different colors, and all that. And then for lunch I had some vegetarian stuff that everybody else said tasted exactly like veal cutlet. There must be something wrong with my mouth."

"Or not," she said. "But what do you make of it all? The stuff they believe." She was smiling as she said this. "Do you dare tell your folks about the sort of weirdos that you're staying with? Assuming you *are* staying, that is."

"Well," said Duncan. He wanted the right tone for what he was going to say. Serious but not sloppy. You could maybe almost say *intimate*. "I think I *would* — and I do plan on staying. But the thing is " — why did he want to tell her this, so much? — "I'm more or less of a free agent. My parents were divorced when I was real little, and I've never had much to do with my dad. And Mom died sort of suddenly, a little while ago. It was an accident. So I live with a neighbor. I'm not exactly *responsible* to anyone, if you know what I mean."

"Jeesh," she said. "I'm sorry." And she really sounded sorry, more or less as if it hurt her, too, to hear about his mother. "That must be pretty rough."

Duncan said, "It could be plenty worse. She's really nice, this neighbor. More like a real good friend. And I'm lucky when it comes to money. There's enough for college. With the scholarship I'm hoping to get," he added.

"I see," she said. "Are you some kind of genius? Or a super jock? Or both?"

That was easier for him to talk about, the stuff he did. He didn't feel he had to press so much, to be mature. He told her who he was, what his credentials were, not making any big deal of it, just stating facts. All it was was *stuff*, a portion of his life; it hadn't made him all that happy.

"The funny thing is," he concluded, "that some of what Christopher told me last night actually made me feel a little better than I'd been feeling. About the future and all that. Once I'd had a chance to chew on it all, for a while."

She turned her head a little, raised an eyebrow. "Yes?" she said. "How so?"

"Oh, I don't know," he said. "It was more the way he got me thinking than most of what he said about Nukismetic Humanism. I can't accept that part about believing there has to be a nuclear war — any kind of war at all, as far as that goes. It seems to me that if you start saying that something's fated to happen, you're almost helping to *make* it happen. You know what I mean? And I certainly don't buy the part about science — or whatever you want to call it — having or finding ways that'll make it possible for certain people to survive a war like that and go on living a decent, ordinary life on this same old decent, ordinary planet."

"So what made you feel better, then?" she asked. "I don't get it."

He gave his little let's-make-fun-of-Duncan sort of laugh. "Well, he said, "it was just him saying — or like, *implying* — that some good can come out of just about anything. It made me think about the flood, back there in the Bible. Don't get me wrong; I'm not some fundamentalist or something. I realize — I *think* I do — that the whole flood story is more of an allegory than actual literal fact, even if there maybe was a real bad flood back then. Well, nowadays, it seems to me, people are really selfish and screwed-up and rotten in different ways, and nothing much works right — just like back then, but different, of course, on account of the times. But that doesn't mean that something can't happen. Something marvelous — miraculous, you might say. Things can change. Even at the last minute."

"Huh," she said. "That's nice. I guess I hope that, too. And it's every bit as plausible as what the Friends are saying. I'm like you: It's always seemed to me that there's a certain similarity between their line of claptrap and the people who go around preaching the end of the world, except the poor fool Friends — " she cut it off and made a little motion with one hand. "Anyway. . . ." She slowed the car and smiled at him. "We're here."

He hadn't paid a lot of attention to the driving they'd been doing. They'd started in a southerly direction; it looked a great deal like the road that he and Sky had first come into town on. But then they'd turned off somewhere, and headed west, toward Lake Champlain. The store was on a dead-end street and almost *in* the lake. Or at least the buildings in back of it were: several enormous, barnlike structures made of cement blocks and sheet metal, each of them supporting NU-HU signs.

"My gosh," he said. "This place is *huge*."

"And getting huger," Caitlin said. "We grow a lot of what we sell, as much of it as possible. Not here, of course, at different places in New York, in Canada, all over. The farms are mostly in spots where Daddy thinks there's likely to be minimum fallout from the particular kinds of blasts he thinks'll go off — if you can believe any of that. But we store a lot of the stuff here, once it's been dried, or canned, or whatever — and there are some — what he calls — *precautions* in the buildings. This place is where we ship from, too: the mail-order part of the business."

"Well, what do *you* do here?" asked Duncan.

"Mostly," she said, "I delegate. That's why we hire such top quality people" — she flipped her hand, palm up, at him — "but my title is" — she cleared her throat — "executive vice-president. Come on."

And she clapped her hand down on his shoulder as she led him into the NU-HU store, just as if he were (he thought) a teammate.

22. HEALTHY APPETITES

Although Duncan and his faithful dog became regular participants in the evening meditation group, they were, for the next half-dozen days, a great deal more involved in the down-to-earth, whole-grain, vitamin-rich (and immensely profitable) operations of NU-HU products. Dunc had a lot to learn about his job — the thing that Christopher tossed off as "playing store" — and it didn't seem to him he was a real fast learner.

Every morning, at more or less the crack of dawn, he and Chris would be awakened by the sound of wind chimes, which was piped to all the rooms — along with static — by the house P.A.

"Tinkle-time," said Christopher, each day, while bobbing quickly up and out of bed, as chipper and as active as a bird. Duncan moved a little slower, but once he got his big feet on the floor, he'd be awake and looking (sort of) forward to the day — its length and shape and possibilities, at least. He felt a whole lot better than at Queen of Peace, even if he wasn't too adept at much of what he did.

All the Friends (and family) who lived there in the house on Willard Street would breakfast in the kitchen or the dining room — both of them enormous, side by side — at six o'clock, five days a week. There was a duty roster posted on the kitchen wall, and everyone took turns at "Set-up," "Cook-up," "Dish-up," and "Clean-up," changing day by day. Duncan was pleased to find that everyone assumed he'd be a total maladroit, so they explained with patient care the way to whisk a group of eggs (you turn the bowl, while doing so), to mix up fresh granola ("with your *hands*, man, with your hands"), and to properly put down a knife (the sharp side *in*) when you are setting tables. Actually, the people there reminded him of Dottie, but a little younger. Like her, they seemed to know a lot of stuff that they would share without a lot of showing off or forcing it, which made them different than some teachers that he'd had. Duncan got the feeling that the Friends were very eager to be different: less competitive, acquisitive, aggressive than society in general. They made comparisons quite often. He wondered how they'd be if there was no society in general for them to be so different than. Like, after this big nuclear occasion they predicted. It was just a passing thought, but still he wondered.

After breakfast, he and Chris and Sky and other people from their breakfast group (no other dogs) would travel to the store by van, where they would open the buildings and organize the stock and start the countless daily tasks peculiar to the health production biz. Sometime in the afternoon, Caitlin would appear, and either head right to her offices (to execute, in good vice-presidential fashion, Duncan guessed) or circulate around and maybe tell him (show him) something new and start him doing something different. Variety was sure the spice of life (along with chili, cumin, curry, nutmeg, and et cetera) at NU-HU.

Every other morning, fresh produce would arrive by truck. Duncan was surprised at that. It meant (it seemed to him, and so he said to Chris) they sold "fresh" produce every *other* day.

"Oh, come now," Christopher replied. " 'Fresh,' in food, is used for anything that isn't rotten. It means that you can eat it and not make a face. Do you have any idea how old the 'strictly fresh' eggs in the average supermarket are? *Weeks* is all, I kid you not. It's true that when people talk about fresh produce, they're imagining Farmer Brown and dewdrops on the ears of corn, *but*" — he put a finger alongside his nose — "I've actually *seen* big semis with out-of-state plates pull up at roadside stands at dawn and toss down *bags* of stuff for junior Brown to sprinkle with a hose. You never *do* know, Dunc. Here, we think the stuff we sell is *recent*, anyway, and not completely mummified by chemicals. But who could guarantee it? Check the guys that bring it in to us sometime. If *they're* organic, I'm Saint Francis of Assisi."

In any case, they organized their produce counters carefully and daily, and Duncan learned to soak the lettuce (always leaf, not iceberg) in cold water in the sink out back, before he put it out. He also learned to tell his russets from his rutabagas, the watercress from the Italian parsley, and that "we never ever go to bed with broccoli, up here."

"A lot of people in these latitudes are vegetarians," said Chris. "You're not, I don't suppose?"

"No," said Duncan. "Neither of us is." Sky wagged, beside him on the floor, as usual. "To tell you the truth, I'm not sure I ever met one before I came up here. What do they eat instead of meat all the time — that stuff we had for dinner my first night?"

Christopher laughed. "Hell no," he said. "There's lots of different kinds of veggies. Some are pretty serious" — he flipped a hand — "and then you have the pizza-Pepsi crowd. But lots of times, it's this stuff here." He waved at the rows of jars and wooden bins that took up one entire wall.

"Brown rice with every kind of bean but jelly: soyas, limas, lentils, basic black, aduki, pinto, kidney, liver, spleen, appendix." Duncan did a double-take, as he was meant to do, he figured. "Organic humor," Christopher explained, and chuckled. "And if not rice, some other good, nutritious grain: whole, stone-ground, steel-cut, or mashed with a rubber spoon. If you eat the right combination of grains and beans you can get as much protein as the Big Bad Wolf on the best day of his life, and with a lot less hassle. It all has to do with amino acids, if you can swallow that." He chuckled again. "But the thing is — you might as well get used to it, because after the big booms go off, the chances are we're going to be existing on that sort of thing for a good long while. A.F.'s got it all figured out. He's got *bunkers*ful of soybeans, for instance, scattered all over the place. They're the stars on Mars, nutrition-wise: far out. A pound of soybeans has as much protein as a pound of Vermont cheddar" — Christopher pantomimed the sign of the cross — "and do you have any idea how much milk it takes to make a pound of cheddar cheese?"

Duncan shook his head and shrugged. The NU-HU store sold lots of cheddar cheese, and also many other kinds including goat and buffalo and maybe pig (thought Duncan).

"Well, neither do I," said Chris, surprisingly, "but it's, like, *gallons*. Now here —"

"Excuse me," said a woman with an eggplant in each hand. "How many *steaks* would you say I can get from these two beauties?" And, facing Christopher, she held up both the purple vegetables.

"No more than ten," he said, emphatically. "That's if you like them thick and juicy, same as I do."

The woman nodded. "Yum," she said. "With wheat germ-sesame breading and a nice tomato sauce with basil and oregano? Now where's that trail mix got to, anyway?"

Chris led her to a barrel of the stuff and scooped her out a paper bag full. When he returned to Duncan's side, he said, "Bless whatever genius coined that name. *Trail* mix. It makes them think they're Lewis and Clark or Dangerous Dan McGrew or Mrs. Brigham Young the twelfth. They put the stuff in little bowls out on the patio and pig it all day long. Then they wonder why they're gaining weight when all they've had all day is health food. *Whale* mix — that'd be more like it: a first-class source of blubber."

When Duncan laughed, Chris looked delighted.

23. BODY SHOP

There was one whole aisle in the center of the store that was given over to the products known as Health and Beauty Aids at any local pharmacy. NU-HU chose to call that section Body Care, and give it this prime space, for reasons Caitlin Fetish laid on Duncan, most emphatically.

"Body care is ball game," she explained. "The source, the letter A, Step One. You think an ayatollah is fanatical? Shake hands with Jane Fonda the first. When I was thirteen, I went away to basketball camp, and the woman in charge of my group was named — you're not going to believe this — Sheila Divine. Well, Sheila Divine had a body *I* could not believe. You know the *Sports Illustrated* swimsuit issue? Well, *that*, and in the flesh; she was completely gorgeous. Muscles, limber, perfect skin and hair" — she wiggled a hand through the air from above her head down to her hips — "the works. Do I have your attention?" She laughed and Duncan rearranged his face. He must have been looking like some kind of a . . . sex maniac, or something.

"She didn't have a beautiful face, necessarily," Caitlin went on, "but the rest of her was so beautiful that it really didn't matter. She was just the healthiest human being that I'd ever seen. And she sat us girls down — I was something of a tuna at that point in time — and told us that our bodies were the only important thing in our lives that we had some real control over. 'Not everyone can be smart or popular or successful or rich, by a long shot,' she told us, 'but almost anyone can be in just terrific *shape*.' She didn't mince words. She said, 'You're going to hear a lot of jive about the problems of being a woman. Well, I'm here to tell you that when you get healthy, all those problems are cut about in two, beginning with the first one, your self-image, and ending with your last one: what the goddam coach is going to call you if you're not.' In perfect shape, that is."

Duncan laughed at that. Those problems were familiar ones, for sure, even for an All-State power forward, male.

"A certain percentage of our customers here," she continued, "are mainly reactors. Some of those have had some health problems in the past, and some just want to do the opposite of what most people are doing. They're reacting, and that's fine — glad to have them with us. But the majority are some degree of Sheila Divines. They're health and body conscious out of conviction; they've made it part of what they do — what they *are*, you could say, even. Okay. Well, we can't do the workouts for them, or make them get the proper sleep and all, but we can offer them decent food" — she gestured at the counters and the coolers and the bins — "and vitamins, and good stuff to put on their skins and their hair." She grinned at him as she said that.

"As far as I'm concerned, this stuff" — she picked up a jar from the shelf — "is just one of those rare, justified paybacks that there are in life. If a person takes the trouble to do hard workouts and get in shape, her body *deserves* some treats. Look." She shoved the jar at him and showed him, once again, that big, wide, kootchy kind of smile, with mischief. "It's got vitamin E and lanolin and all sorts of good stuff in it. You should try it, or even try it on a friend. Until you have, you ain't felt nothing yet, believe me."

Duncan made a mouth and nodded, rubbed his jaw for something serious to do. "Uh, *yes*," he said. "Looks good." He knew she was teasing him — not *being* a tease, but teasing, which was different. But he'd never been teased by a girl her age before — assuming that's what it was, as he did — and he was a long way from knowing how to handle it.

"I saw you running when I left for school the other day," she said, now serious again. "So I know you know what I'm talking about. Plus your being a player. And that's what I was thinking. We have a hoop up on the carriage house — did you know that?" He shook his head. "Well, if you want to shoot around when I'm not home any time, you can borrow my ball. And maybe sometimes we can work out together, even play a little one-on-one. Not that I'm in your league." And she flapped her eyebrows at him. He made a face. She punched him on the arm.

"Come on," she said. "I'll show you out back now."

What was out back were the big buildings, which served the company as storehouses, as the offices and distribution center for the mail-order part of the business, and as the place where certain of the health products were mixed, and jarred, and bottled.

"Parts of this, you'll never have a thing to do with," she explained. "The rooms where we put the vitamins together, or age the cheeses in — we have to keep as sterile an atmosphere as possible in them. So only a particular group of workers goes in there, wearing special clothes and all that. But you'll hit some of the other jobs before you leave, probably — orders, loading, different stuff. We find it keeps people from getting stale, if they move around some."

"Well, that'd probably be good for me," Duncan said. "I feel like such a doofus out in the store. I know it's just the first week, but still. Chris does all this pouring and slicing and weighing routine without ever making any sort of mess *and* more or less entertaining the customers at the same time, where I'm all thumbs, and spilling this, and knocking over that, and not having the slightest idea which herbs they ought to put in the rat-tat-twee, or whatever it's called. Sky does a lot better with the customers than I do. He smiles and wags his tail and shakes their hands, and they tell him to have a nice day and everything. But me, I'm really not doing the program a whole hell of a lot of good, so far."

She laughed. "You'll get the hang of it," she said. "Probably. Chris is a natural; he's just a fantastic storekeeper. And Sky — the guy's one of those rare characters that everybody likes. Takes all kinds, y'know." And she shook her head and made a little clucking sound.

"Actually," she said, "to maybe soothe your culture shock a little . . . I've got a job up at the house I need someone to help with, for a day or two. It's painting. How are you at that?"

"Jesus," Duncan said. "I'd probably be terrible." It was disgusting to realize — he realized — how few things he actually did know how to do, with any sort of skill. "I've never painted anything except a chair for my room. This chair my mother bought at some garage sale for my desk, and I wanted it red instead of sort of mold-colored. I ended up getting little red spots all over the wall. Like chicken pox, kind of."

"Well, that's okay," she said. "Because it's actually *walls* I want you to do. Some rooms on the second floor. And being tall will make it easier. You want to try it? Starting after breakfast Monday morning? I can get you started, before I leave for school."

And that was how it happened Duncan got enrolled in chromotherapy — a minicourse, you might say. And also learned the layout of the Fetishes' apartment, which is to say the second floor, on Willard Street.

24. PAINT JOB

"Ah-*bah*— hah, hah," said Abraham Fetish loudly, and then less loudly, as he emerged from his bathroom at 6:52 A.M., bringing with him odors, like bay rum, for (pleasant) instance. Duncan was fairly sure that the last two "hah"s were stall words, which Fetish used to make a friendly sound, while groping for his name.

"So, here you come a-muralling, eh . . . Stuart?" the friendliest of all the Friends inquired. His mind had resurrected something: This tall boy had a Scottish name. His eyes provided the further fact that he was carrying all manner of painter's paraphernalia, and was following his daughter Caitlin down the hall. "A little chiaroscuro in the mahster bedroom, maybe? She's threatened me with this for weeks and weeks. 'The woman schemes and combs her silken fleece by day, but spins it into cord at night.' Vitamins 8, 16. But stop, and let me see the color scheme she's chosen. 'Dwell not in walls that clash with fingernails or set the teeth to gnash.' Sententians 43, verses 5 and 6."

Duncan stopped, set down his ladder and the drop cloths, and started to pry the top off the can that he'd been holding.

"You don't have to do that," Caitlin said. "They put a color sample on the front. See, Daddy? It's an awfully nice light blue. Sort of between a slate and a summer sky. And the trim'll be royal blue; it'll really be striking."

Fetish shot his eyebrows up and struck himself a smart one on the forehead. "Perfecto!" he exclaimed. "And an excellent environment for both of you to work in, lads," he said, addressing Sky and Duncan. "The color aura that you want is very much like this, though not so flat, of course. More *liquid*, glisteny, eh . . . *Malcolm*, isn't it?"

"Duncan, sir," said Duncan.

"Duncan-Duncan-Duncan — yes, of course," said Fetish. "I knew it all along." He squinted at the boy. "Right now — just as a point of reference — your aura's greenish-yellow-brown, with just an underlay of rose. There's lots of cool in you to start with, glad to say. Every time I've seen you, it's been there. Now this one here's another story." He hunkered down and patted Sky. "All full of orange-reds and purples, aren't we?" he crooned. "A loosely woven *tweed* of warmth and honesty. Commitment. A dog among dogs, sir. 'Fido is a man's best friend, but Flora's great for. . . .' Folderol 18, line 12."

"Okay, Dad — right," said Caitlin. "But we've got to get started now, or I'll be late for class, and I know you're probably — "

"Indeed I am," her father said. "Montpelier." He threw a bear hug on his daughter, and big as she was, he still enveloped her, entirely. "Have a dandy daub there, Duncan, and I'll see you both at dinner." He headed for the stairs.

Caitlin heaved a sigh and beckoned Duncan farther down the wide main hall. When they'd first gotten to the second floor, she'd explained how the space up there was organized and shared. Straight across the hall from the stairs was a guest room with bath. That was neutral territory. But everything to the right — which was about two thirds of the floor — was basically her father's, and everything to the left was hers. He had an enormous office, just beyond his bath and bedroom, on the east side of the hall, and on the other side — the stair side — a living room connected to a kitchenette. Caitlin's section consisted of a bedroom and bath, a tiny sitting room, and a study half the size of Abraham's.

"Let's start in his office," Caitlin said. "No, come to think of it, better do the bedroom first, and maybe it won't stink too bad by sundown. And, anyway, we know he spends at least eight hours there, each day. Though I sort of doubt that it works in the dark, or while someone's sleeping . . . or would it?" She seemed to be talking to herself toward the end of that.

She chewed a thumbtip. But Duncan didn't stand on ceremony; he had his own concerns.

"Works?" he said. "What *works*? Is there something in this paint, or something?" Ever since Ben had told him stories about them putting saltpeter in the food at his brother's school, and in prisons, he'd been a little . . . defensive, you could say, about any possible attacks on his equipment, or his motives, even. Was there something in this paint that Caitlin wanted her father to inhale (but maybe not to smell) that would affect him, too?

"Of course there is," she said. She took the screwdriver from his breast pocket and pried open one of the cans. "You're looking at it. Color. People have known about this stuff for centuries — that it could do things, change things. But because what happened couldn't be explained and wasn't understood, they filed it under M, for magic. But here's a simple F, for fact. Different colors make you feel a lot of different ways. Back in the 1800's there were guys who'd do curing with colors — chromotherapy, they called it. Classy, eh? They'd bathe the patient in a different color light, depending. Cancer, constipation, or whatever — they didn't give a *hoo*-rah. Not knowing what was really up, they tried to work on everything. The scatter-gun approach."

She laughed. "Lisle," she said, "this guy I hang around with, is a doctor, or about to be. He claims that today's photobiologists — that's chromotherapists in double knits and with a PhD — are looking for the magic bullet and are full of it. Lisle knows more than God, of course. Actually, he just tries to act that way. Up in Med School, they have classes in How-To-Make-Everyone-Who-Isn't-a-Doctor-Feel-Like-a-Total-Jerk. Required every year. Otherwise the nurses, who actually deal with a lot of sick people, would walk all over them. That's what I tell him, anyway."

Duncan said, "You mean you think colors do . . . *do* things to people?"

She nodded. "I'm pretty sure of it. Lisle thinks the claims are totally inflated and that a lot of the studies are poorly conceived, but I think he's just banging his lips and keeping the defensive platoon on the field. A lot of MD's still lump psychologists with alchemists, anyway. Without going into all the vulgar details, we think that color at least contributes to mood, and therefore to the psychosomatic component in so much disease, and probably also has a direct physiolial effect, by way of the pituitary and pineal glands."

Duncan thought that maybe he should whistle, so he did. "Huh," he added onto that. "So what are you trying to do to your father? Has he got something wrong with him?"

Caitlin looked at him and raised an eyebrow. "You *might* say that," she said. "I'd like to get his blood pressure down, for one thing. And maybe sort of mellow him out, in general. There might be a lot more violence in the guy than meets the eye — you know? If you ask me, the whole idea of Nukismetic Humanism is aggressive as hell, no matter what they like to say about their calm, nonviolent, vegged-out ways. 'Those cunning little Nookies,' Lisle's been known to call them. You can imagine what he thinks of this houseful that we've got. *I* think they're harmless enough, but I also think they may be suppressing some really aggressive feelings, by more or less substituting this great nuclear event of theirs. They can appear to be peaceful, passive folk and lovers of all humankind who aren't the least bit mad at the hundreds of millions of other people who are lousing up their Spaceship Earth by insisting on existing. And all the time they're really raging inside. I hope that isn't true of my father, but if it is, I'd just as soon he doesn't stay that way.

"The thing with Daddy is," she said, "that I'm not a hundred percent sure he believes it anyway. All the NU-HU philosophic stuff. Could be it's all jive; he's got a lot of that in him, as *possibly* you've noticed. But just in case he does believe it . . . why not give this color stuff a try? Plus, the rooms on this floor need painting anyway. When we're through with his, I think I'd like to do mine, too. Bubble-gum pink. That's another of the passive colors. Football coaches have been using it in visiting team's locker rooms. Meant to turn the opposition into lamby-pies. But somehow I couldn't quite see it for Daddy."

Duncan shook his head and smiled, expressing both confusion and agreement.

"Now, look," said Caitlin. With which, in whirlwind style, she showed him how to use the drop cloths and the roller pan, the rollers and the brush.

"Never mind the trim today," she said. "Maybe I'll do that myself — it's slightly trickier, in terms of drip. And when you finish here, go right on to his living room, okay? Then the kitchen, bath, and office, in that order. Of course you won't do all of that today, not even close. Oh — and I've got some gray carpeting coming in, too, when the painting's all done. That'll make the rooms *exactly* like the ones in the schoolroom up in Edmonton, at this children's center, where they did the original experiment. The results with the kids up there were amazing, even two blind ones, can you believe it? Before we know it, the guy'll probably be stretched out on the road to Seabrook, or something. Boy, how'd you like to have to pick *him* up, if you were a trooper?" She gave herself a shake. "Anyway. You all set, now? I'll see you maybe two . . . or three o'clock, the latest. And thanks a million, Dunc." She dropped down on one knee to shake with Sky. "Bye-bye, Sky, sweetheart," she said dotingly, and kissed him on the muzzle. "You have a *real* nice day, dear."

She rolled her eyes at Duncan then, and made her exit, laughing.

Sky hung around until he got a good whiff of the paint. Then he padded down the hall and jumped onto Caitlin's bed. He knew he'd get a call when it was time to eat, or run.

25. CHECKING IN (1)

By the time the telephone in the booth by the edge of the park started to ring, Dottie Michalis had just about convinced herself that it was never going to do that — or maybe even couldn't. That Duncan Banigan was never going to call — or maybe even couldn't. After all, it *was* the tenth day after he'd left New Jersey, even if it (also) was only the sixth weekday on which she'd come to lunch, as usual, beside the public phone booth in the park. He'd left on a Friday, and this was Monday, once again: the second one he'd been away, somewhere.

Dottie Michalis had never been the worrying kind (she would have said), nor one to have a lot of expectations. So she wasn't at all sure why her heart jumped straight up into her throat when the phone rang, and why she had to wonder for a moment, when she'd risen from the bench, if her legs would carry her across the sidewalk.

"Dottie! Hi! It's me! Old Duncan." He sounded near, not far, and fine. "Sorry I couldn't call before. I'm in Vermont all right. How are you?"

"Great," she managed, breathless. "It's good to hear your voice. You almost had me worried." Saying that made her laugh, and suddenly the tightness in her chest was gone. She took a good deep breath. "You bastard. You *did* have me worried, you know that? What's the story, anyway? Is everything okay?"

"Absolutely," Duncan said. "The thing is — I have this job, and where I was working last week, I couldn't use the phone, long distance, and there weren't any phone booths around. But anyway. I found out why Brian wanted me to come up here. There's this group of people — almost like a cult, you might say — called the Nukismetic Humanists. A little strange, but really friendly. They're the ones who've given me my job, and a place to stay, and everything."

"So they don't . . . it doesn't have anything to do with what happened down here?" she asked.

"No, not at all," he said quickly, and he could hear her make a sound, a kind of sigh. "They're actually almost pacifists, and very clean livers. They have a huge health food business. I don't have to actually join or anything, either, but some of the stuff they do is kind of interesting. The head of it's this huge guy who's trying to teach me to meditate and change the color of my *aura*? You know what one of those is?" He heard her go uh-huh. "And his daughter's sort of head of the health food part. She's older than me and she used to play in the WBL and she's crazy about Sky. She's about six-one, you should see her. She's a graduate student at the University up here."

"Huh," Dottie said. "Terry's been coming over every day, just about. It'd be really nice if you could write her, or get in touch with her somehow. But maybe you shouldn't try just yet."

"No?" He really did seem happy, Dottie thought. Kids were amazing. He sounded a lot different than just before he left. "Why not?" he said. "You think the cops'd tap the Bissonette's phone, too? Or check on their mail? They're all that anxious to know where I am?"

"Well," said Dottie, "I don't know. Not necessarily the police. There've been some real strange things happening. Phone calls — for you. A man with an accent who wouldn't give his name. And I think someone's going through our mail, while I'm still at work. I know how Mr. Burke puts it in the box, always the same way. And a couple of times it's been different, upside down. And, well, someone got into your mother's . . . into your house."

"What?" said Duncan. "Somebody broke into the house? What for? Did they steal anything?"

"I don't know," Dottie said. "I couldn't really tell. Nothing obvious, anyway. I guess they were looking for something. Mostly in your room and Brian's. All the drawers were opened, and some of your stuff got scattered around."

Duncan groaned. "Oh, no," he said. "Sounds like a real mess. Did you call the cops?" He was trying to think if there was anything in his room he wouldn't want someone to look at. He *had* kept a journal for a while, when he and Terry were first starting to get serious. . . .

"Yes," she said. "I decided to just act normal. Seeing as we agreed I should tell them you were missing, it seemed logical to call them about this."

"Right," said Duncan. "So what'd they do?"

"Not a whole lot," she said. "They asked me if I'd heard from you, and went through the same routine about how if you called I should find out where you were and get in touch with them, right away. I guess you're listed as a runaway. Then one of them asked me if I thought you were in a position to call; that's an exact quote: 'in a position to call.' I asked him what that was supposed to mean, and he said, oh, he didn't know, but if *he* was a friend of yours, he'd be getting a little concerned, 'about now.' Obviously, the guy was trying to scare me, I thought. Like, in case I was holding anything back."

"Boy," said Duncan. "That stinks. But I'll tell you this much. What all that makes me feel is that the best thing for me to do right now is stay exactly where I am. Let them think I'm dead, if they want to. There's no problem with my staying here, for as long as I want, almost. I told them I was on an independent study project from school, so they wouldn't think it was funny if I stayed right up till June."

"Maybe that would be best," said Dottie. It was ridiculous, how mixed up she felt. "Do you want me to say anything to Terry?"

"Sure," he said. "Just tell her I'm fine, and feeling a lot better, in some ways. And make sure she understands why I can't get in touch, and why I ought to stay here for now. *You* know. And tell her not to worry, okay?"

He paused. She didn't say anything.

"Or you either," he said. "I don't want you to worry either."

She still didn't speak.

"I know it might seem a little strange for me to be way off up here and not *doing* anything. But . . . I don't know, it still seems like there isn't anything I *can* do, except try to get my head together, and maybe in the meantime the cops'll find the people who did it, and we can get back to normal. Okay? Okay, Dottie?"

"Sure, I guess so," she said. "I think I'm just feeling a little weird about all the stuff that's been happening. I'm glad you're far away, actually. And I'm really happy you called."

"Me, too," he said. "And I'll call again in a week or so — maybe next Monday, if I can. And if it's not raining." He laughed.

"Okay," said Dottie. "Good. You just take care of yourself."

"You bet," he said. "And thanks for everything, Dottie. I'm really sorry to have dragged you into all this." That sounded ridiculous to him, as if they were talking about some minor misunderstanding, instead of . . . what had happened, *was* happening. But he felt so far from where she was, so strange. It was almost as if he had another life now, like college would be, but even more so. "So give my love to Terry, too, all right?" he said. "Bye-bye."

"Bye, Dunc," she said, and slowly hung up the receiver. She felt both better and worse than when he left, she realized.

After he hung up, Duncan stood inside the phone booth for a moment, worrying. He wondered if maybe he wasn't being the worst son, the worst brother, the worst coward in the history of the world. But still he couldn't think of anything else to *do*. Much better to leave the doing to the cops; they had the training; he was just a kid. The only thing that he felt was wrong — well, perhaps not *wrong*, but inappropriate — was this: He shouldn't be enjoying life so much — not yet — be having quite so good a time, while Dottie there, and Terry, had all sorts of hassles, strains, and worries. But yet, this wasn't his idea; it was Brian's. He was just doing what his older brother'd said to. There couldn't be a whole lot wrong with that.

He hustled back to Willard Street, with Sky right by his side.

26. LISLE HARDAWAY

Lisle Hardaway (soon to be MD) liked to wave hello to people in the halls or on the street, and when he did, he'd raise his index finger to about head height, and then give it one or two quick shakes in the direction of the person being greeted. The gesture was much the same as the one that many students make at sports events these days, when they're claiming that their team is great — preeminent, in fact. "We're Number One," he seemed to signal, as he walked the road of life.

Lisle may not have been a king, or Pope, but still the royal "we" was not entirely inappropriate. He was outstanding in a lot of ways: an honor student from Grade One, captain of his college soccer team; he almost always looked as if he'd just been to the barber shop, and then had scrubbed himself to pink perfection in a scalding, soapy shower.

Soon, of course, he'd be (what else?) a surgeon — an intern matched with (well, where else?) his first-choice hospital.

The only thing that bothered him about his life was that he didn't have a live-in girl friend, namely Caitlin Fetish. They'd been going out together for a good two years, enjoyed each other's company, used such words as *love*, and gone to bed together. Lisle had more or less assumed they would be married, maybe once he'd opened an office of his own, and until then . . . he thought that they should live together.

In Lisle Hardaway's opinion, Caitlin Fetish was just about the perfect girl for him. She was smart; good-looking; healthy, with a straight spine; wore nice clothes; and had no outrageous chemical addictions. Her ancestry was Lebanese and Finnish, where he was almost purely Celtic: great, genetically, for children. On top of that she didn't cook a lot of spicy food or ask to go to movies where the actors spoke Hungarian. She even had the independence and the self-sufficiency to take the role of doctor's wife and go with it (English translation: She didn't mind being left alone for long periods of time); she got to sleep and woke up easily, and wasn't in the least bit grouchy or demanding. And, like almost everyone he'd met in life so far, she seemed to get along with him.

The reasons that Lisle Hardaway had to put that "just about" in there, whenever he stopped to consider what a perfect *woman* Caitlin Fetish was for him — he was training himself not to think *girl*, and managed to do so, one time out of three at least — was that he wasn't a hundred percent sure they were compatible. In certain ways, that is. There was, for instance, first of all, that "work" of hers. Not the health food store, the other stuff. It really did appear she meant to be a clinical psychologist. And try as he might, Lisle Hardaway could not see that *at all*.

He wanted to be fair, God knew (*he* knew). In the interest of fairness, he'd even very carefully gone through the lists of people in his class, and also in the class before his, who'd chosen, as their specialty, psychiatry. Psychiatrists were something like clinical psychologists, but being doctors, better. And almost all the people who'd chosen to be *them* were (in Lisle's opinion) slightly weird, at least. It was his theory, in fact, that if you chose to be a shrink, it almost had to be because you wondered what the hell was wrong with *you*. And rightly so. Just for an example: He was pretty sure — he'd overheard it in the locker room — that two of the people in the class ahead of him who were going to be shrinks were also gay. As Lisle often said, he was as open-minded as the next guy, but still; he *knew* those people wondered. Also: Three of the *women* in his own class were going to be shrinks, plus the guy who'd supposedly fainted on his first day in the anatomy lab, and the dude with the incredible acne, and the one who'd lived on an *ashram*, for God's sake. This was not what Lisle would call a *muy* impressive group of people.

Now, granted, clinical psychologists *were* a different breed of cat. Less real knowledge of the human body and its functions, lots and lots more beards; unable to prescribe drugs, they couldn't treat the total patient. And what they *did* do seemed to Lisle to be ridiculous, very near dishonest. Those people, as he understood it, charged the public great humongous fees for doing next to nothing — except smoking smelly pipes and repeating, in some shorter form, whatever it was that their loony "client" had just said to them. As:

> *Client:* "I can remember when I was just an infant, lying in her arms, and hearing Mother say to me: 'You suck. You *really* suck, you know that?'"
>
> *Clinical Psychologist:* "You *knew* your mother hated you."

But in addition to Lisle Hardaway's feelings about psychiatrists and clinical psychologists, there was also something else. Lisle was a little — very slightly, mind you — worried about whether he and Caitlin were . . . well, *physically* compatible. He wasn't *that* experienced, so it was hard to say, but, see, the thing was this: The sex they'd had had been enjoyable, but he wasn't sure that it was All That Great, the way he knew it *should* be — at least according to the guy (the *psychiatrist*, as a matter of shameful fact) who'd led his

JULIAN F. THOMPSON

Human Sexuality Seminar up at the Med School, first year. Sure, the guy was plenty weird all right, but he did seem to be pretty well (maybe even a little *too* well) informed, sex-wise, and he'd made it very clear that if it wasn't All That Great, you really ought to Do Something About It, which would probably involve seeing a psychiatrist! But that (of course) was out of the question. It seemed to Lisle that if things didn't change (after they'd been living together for a while), it would almost be easier and better to get another girl (make that *woman*) rather than do anything else. Compatible, he thought, might very well be born, not made, and it probably depended more than anything on the woman herself — how uptight she was, and so on. A lot of girls were very iffy when it came to sex, he'd always known.

But he didn't even like to think about breaking up with Caitlin. They really were so good together, such a good match. Things would probably iron themselves out, in time, once they started living together. Chances (even) were she wouldn't even practice her psychology routine, once she started having babies.

Lisle would have been surprised and horrified if he had know that Caitlin Fetish had a few reservations about their relationship, too. She hadn't taken the Human Sexuality Seminar up at the Med School, so although she, too, felt their sex life might be better, it hadn't occurred to her to either blame somebody or Do Something About It. Her decision was very much like his, in any case: to simply wait and see; she was pretty sure that they'd be a whole lot better in bed once (or if) she was committed to him much more deeply than she was, and he came on as slightly less . . . professional. Caitlin had felt for some time that she "loved" Lisle Hardaway, but she wasn't about to start living with him until she was totally convinced she wouldn't want to change him if she could.

27. HERD BULLS

Sky and Duncan, from their different rooms, heard Caitlin in the hall, partly because she was singing "Good-bye, Old Paint" (the Western song) and partly because she seemed to be taking twice as many footsteps as were necessary. Sky hopped down off her bed and went to greet her and investigate, which meant he got to meet Lisle Hardaway before Duncan did. To Sky's way of thinking, that wasn't any great event; Lisle tried to pat him with just the palm of his hand, no fingers. As a pat, it was about a one point five; Dunc and Caitlin gave him eights when they were *eating*, for gosh sake.

Duncan fared a little better.

"Duncan, this is Lisle," said Caitlin. "Lisle meet Duncan."

He came down from the ladder, changing hands on the roller and wiping the right one on his jeans. Lisle had no alternative but to shake (including fingers) and to flash the pearly whites — both of which he did with practiced ease.

"It's a pleasure," Lisle proclaimed. "Katy's told me all about you. I wish I'd had the chance to do this sort of thing, when I was back in high school." Duncan wondered, fleetingly, if the guy could possibly be referring to painting a wall with a roller.

In point of actual fact, Lisle Hardaway would not have left the ego-building comfort of his A.P. -honors classes at the most selective prep school in the country for all the experiences this side of Cathay, but setting the patient at ease came a long way ahead of absolute, literal honesty, in his opinion-practice. His mind was rapidly taking note of the fact that the subject was a post-pubescent male Caucasian mesomorph with clear skin, a steady eye, and had a good three inches on him.

"Well," said Duncan, who hadn't missed that "Katy", "I'm afraid I'm getting a lot more out of the whole deal than the Fetishes are, so far. I'm no great shakes with one of these — oops!" He just snagged a drip from the roller before it fell on the rug. He put the roller in the pan and wiped his hand on a rag, this time.

"I think it's looking *great*," said Caitlin. "Such an improvement over that sunshine yellow — sun*set* yellow, better — or whatever it was." She turned to

Lisle. "We're using the colors from that Edmonton experiment I told you about? The one at the school for handicapped kids? Where they got the seventeen percent decline in their mean systolic blood pressure?"

"Oh, yes," he said. "Wasn't that the place where they also gave the kids nothing to eat but chopped liver and brewer's yeast sandwiches on wheat germ bread, and all of them turned out to be Wayne Gretzky?"

"Very funny," Caitlin said. And then, to Duncan, "Lisle, like surgeons everywhere, prefers to operate. His second choice'd be drugs: push a little chemical from his enormous and *in*delicate-essen. Who cares about a simple side effect? A minor — mere — dependency? In his book — a most *extremely* limited edition, I might add — vitamin and nutritional therapies are akin to casting bones or boiling bats' wings in the urine of a pregnant mare. He'd rather they should pop a pill — a little Valium, m'deah? — than eat a lot of good B vitamins."

Lisle Hardaway put up protesting palms. "Did *I* say that? Did I *ever* say a thing like that? Actually, a well-poached bat wing is a favorite snack of mine, right up there with the broiled iguana skins, *au gratin*."

Matching her routine, he turned to Duncan. "You may have noticed: Here at Nookie House, the Gideons don't stand a chance. Instead it's Saint Adelle on every bedside table, or the blessed Linus Pauling. From a strictly scientific point of view, their claims are no more fanciful than the writings of the Brothers

Grimm, I don't suppose — but not a great deal less, either. Here's what I say, Duncan. I haven't got the slightest doubt that good father Abraham will feel a little better in his newly painted suite, but not — alas — because it's colored blue or gray. He'll feel better because of this new evidence of *caring*, on his lovely daughter's part — and also yours, I guess — and because at last the place is clean and free of mold. Bacteria, my dear, *bacteria*."

He turned and took Caitlin Fetish's cheek between his thumb and forefinger and gave it a good tweaking. "Things that, unlike your ravishing and mind-destroying beauty, can be seen under a *micro*scope!"

Caitlin batted the offending hand away. "Get outta here," she said. "Now I know what Galileo felt like, you scientific inquisitionist."

"Can you imagine what it'd be like, living with a creep like this?" she said to Duncan. "Smart me, for having none of his indecent propositions." But Duncan got the feeling that her outrage wasn't real, but part of a routine, a part of their relationship. Almost an intimate part.

"The thing is," she went on, "*he* couldn't possibly imagine it — and you know why? No imagination whatsoever. That's the trouble with you, young Doc Hardaway — you ain't got no imagination what-so-ever." And she swatted him three times as she said that, those three on the shoulder, not too hard.

Lisle Hardaway laughed, the good sport's sound. He didn't like it when that word came up: imagination. His English teacher back in prep school had kept asking him for some — in addition to the facts of who said what to whom, in *Silas Marner*. His lack of it —*supposedly*— had kept him from high honors in the course. And, during the Human Sexuality Seminar at Med School, he'd wondered a couple of times if possibly his lovemaking could be described as unimaginative. Well, if so, it was a conscious choice, he told himself. Integrity was a lot more important than mirrors and trapezes to a medical professional.

"Well," said Caitlin, once again to Duncan. "I've got to drop off Quincy, Junior, at St. Nowhere, and then get down and mind the store awhile. I should be back a little after five, so I'll see you then, if you're still at it."

"Good to have met you, Duncan," Lisle insisted, as they left. Duncan checked his watch: two-thirty. He'd work . . . oh, say three hours more or so, he figured.

28. CHECKING IN (2)

You may have noticed that the people who are closest to you are able to get you angrier than anyone else. First of all, they know how. And secondly, they have the power to affect you more; the things they do — no question about it — *matter*.

Abraham Fetish would have agreed with all of the above; Mister Carlo, at regular intervals, had always made him perfectly furious.

"I can drive him up the mall, like that," Mister Carlo also might have said, and snapped his fingers in the air; probably he might have chuckled, too. "He flies smack into a tower of rage," he might have added. Mister Carlo's grasp of American idioms was still, at best, approximate.

On the particular occasion you're getting set to read about, things were at their all-time worst, between them.

"You haven't found him *yet*?" Fetish shrieked into the telephone. "You dolt! You nincompoop! How could I ever have been fool enough to assign you to New Jersey in the first place? 'Send not the rutting goat to dally with the llama.' Shenanigans 18, verse 3. Why *haven't* you?"

"I haven't 'cause I haven't," Mister Carlo screamed right back. "Every day, since I got back, I'm out es-searching. I'm es-searching like a five-tooth crone. Why haven't I? I tell you why. He ain't no place I look, tha's why!"

"Ooosh," cried Fetish, making of the sound part growl, part moan (a groan?). "Well, look some other places then. A boy that age just doesn't disappear." Fetish didn't read the papers much, apparently, or hang around in New York City. "You simply have to find him. Every day he isn't found — he isn't dealt with — brings us closer to perdition. I'm talking of our *lives*, our *freedom*. Dare I say — you wretch! — our very *souls*?"

Mister Carlo made a sound that could have been a sob, and Fetish knew at once he'd gone too far.

"Hey, Abe," said Mister Carlo in a quiet voice. "Onfair. You know is not my fault, no more'n yours. I do my best. Since I got back to town, I been tryin' ever-thing that I can think of. Jay's in, jay's out, I es-search for any kinda clue to where he is. I call up ona phone; I hang aroun' the lady's house, the girl frien's house, the boyfrien's house, the school. I look in all the letter boxes; I even wiggle in the house he useta live in. Nuttin'. I know you're glowin' your top up there, but how you think I'm feelin'? Happy? Satisfied? Apiece?"

Fetish cleared his throat. "You're right, of course," he said. "I'm sorry, Carlo; I'm acting very badly. 'If you can't afford the steaks, get out of the chophouse.' Provenders, chapter 6, line 33. It's not a pretty business we're involved in."

"I keep on lookin', Abe," said Mister Carlo, "but I'm afraid he's blown the soup. I never shoulda run away two weeks, big chicken. Or I shoulda hooked my chances at the wake."

Fetish, tight-lipped, shook his head, a good two hundred fifty miles away, or more. "I can't blame you for not doing it then, Carlo. You'd never have gotten out of that room; it just wasn't the time. Look. If nothing turns up in two-three days, you come on home. We'll put our heads together. I worry more for Caitlin than for me. 'When the flood runs over stinker's dam, blood is quicker than water.' Cutpurse, 47."

Mister Carlo nodded grimly as they both hung up. He thought he'd heard that one before.

29. ONE-ON-ONE

Some lanky girls appear to be all wrists and elbows, awkward angles. Although they fold their arms, and duck their heads, and try to walk in shorter steps, and keep their shoulders rounded . . . well, they still stand out. *Stick* out. People have to sneak a second look, to see if they've got problems, or what.

Caitlin Fetish never went that route. Going down the halls in high school, she would stride and glide, her shoulders back, her arms and long braid swinging. Often, she would jump and touch a spot high up the wall, the molding or a transom's top for instance, the border of an exit sign. All through the school she had these lucky spots; touching them would help the world work right, the way she liked it to.

Most days she wore boys' corduroys. They had the length of leg she needed, and fit her tight around a butt made hard and round by all the leaping that she did. You see that same behind on dancers, skaters, sprinters, gymnasts; like her, they have to work for it. Caitlin used to hop up this long set of concrete steps, in front of a neighbor's house — first on her left foot, then on her right, fifty trips each leg. She did it for the sake of basketball, rather than her ass, not to say the body changes weren't welcome. She also wore her father's huge old sweaters, V-necked cashmeres in the softest tans and greens and grays, the arms pushed up, the necks a bit askew, sometimes. She liked the way the sweaters felt against her skin — the swing of them, they were so big, so loose and easy. But mostly she wore turtlenecks or leotards as well, more on account of her girl friends than the boys. Some things weren't worth the hassle, and school was only part of life. She liked being small-breasted and only wore a bra on the basketball court; the coaches said they had to, no exceptions.

Caitlin always talked in class; she expected to be interested, not bored. That was mostly because her father was interesting, and she had had him to herself since she was eight. Duncan's fantasy had been correct: Her mother *had* died young, a victim of her times, a very modern cancer. So Caitlin had been served a double-dip of love by Abraham, for almost all her life. He'd mothered her and fathered her, and though he didn't always say "You may," he never said "You can't." The combination of his attitude and the skills she was prepared to cultivate gave her a rather easy adolescence. She listened (then *and* now) to all the doubts and fears and insecurities her friends would worry over, but she didn't feel a lot of them herself. In fact, her reasons for becoming a psychologist were just the opposite of those Lisle Hardaway assumed his classmates had — the ones who planned to be psychiatrists. She *knew* she wasn't really weird, and thought she might be useful.

Given all the ways she was, it figured she would like Duncan Banigan, but not anatomize her liking much. He seemed to be a member of her tribe: tall, clean, athletic, smart enough, independent, a dog lover, modest, hard-working. And — yeah, sure, why not? — he obviously liked her. If her father hadn't put the T-bird up on blocks, she might have had a brother something like this boy — but only *something*. This wasn't her brother. She thought he had the best looking hands she'd ever seen on a guy.

She definitely could shoot the basketball. Duncan saw that right away. She had a smooth release, a lovely follow-through — her palm turned out, her thumb straight down, almost. A lovely follow-through made (from a certain standpoint) even lovelier when she unzipped, and then took off, the warm-up jacket she'd been wearing. Her T-shirt, which was gray, said STARS on it; she kept her dark blue slender sweat pants on, but pulled the zippers at the ankles for about six inches. The bottoms of her pant legs flipped and flopped each time she jumped; her sneakers were white high-tops, Pumas.

They played some games of Round-the-World, a game in which you shoot the ball from each of seven spots, starting in one corner of the court and moving out around the key, to end up in the other corner; the shots are, maybe, sixteen-to-eighteen footers. If you make your first shot, you move on; if you miss, you have the choice of trying it again or not, but if you take the second try and miss it, you have to go back to the start on your next turn. In macho Round-the-World, the kind that Duncan played at home, you *always* took the second shot, but here he was prepared to make adjustments in his game, depending.

She made her first four shots, all silk-smooth jumpers, hitting nothing more than cord. But when she missed the fifth, she said, "I think I'll stay," and tossed the ball to him. Of course he missed the very first one that he tried, went again, and made it, then hit the next four straight before he missed one, off the iron, in and out. When in Rome . . . , he thought, and also chose to stay, not risk the second shot. And so she ran the rest on him and cackled, "One for me." From that point on, they both took all the risk shots, making them more often than they missed. She kept the edge that first game gave her, nipped him eight to seven.

"Okay," she said, at that point. "How about a little one-on-one? We'll play the first one even, just to set my handicap, okay? But you really have to try, you promise?"

Sure. He nodded. Fine.

She slipped her sweat pants off. The shorts were not the silk that he'd imagined — just plain dark navy blue, and cotton. Totally uninteresting — uh-huh. She had a tight elastic bandage on one knee. They threw fingers for the ball; she won.

Dunc had never played against a girl before, not one-on-one, that is. And the girls he *had* played with, just hackers' games, were more inclined to laugh and squeal than hand-check him, and force him to his left, or come right at him with their dribble, only to reverse and pivot smoothly off him to the hoop. And then — oh, yes — then *laugh*.

Before a lot of minutes passed, Duncan had the situation sized up this way: size and strength were clearly on his side; he was a better leaper, if not a quicker one; she could shoot with him, was very slick, had great anticipation (better than his own) — and tricks, she had a bagful.

They went right at each other. Duncan found that he'd forget she was a girl for little action-spurts of time, remembering when someone scored, or if he fouled her hard enough to hurt. When he was playing defense, he put his hands on her as if she were a guy, another player. And she returned the favor. They both called fouls against themselves.

One time, she grabbed the bottom of his shorts — fingers up the outside of one leg — the instant he went up to snare a rebound. Firmly in her grip, the shorts stayed where they were, and he jumped out of them. He came down with the ball all right, but with his pants down, too, almost to his knees. She laughed, completely unembarrassed, and he did the same — at least the laughing part. He yanked them up.

140

"I guess that was a foul," she said.

"My ball," he answered, clutching it. She whacked him on the butt and nodded. They kept on playing.

It was a good game. They didn't keep score after all, but he felt that he was winning, not by much, and mostly just because he got the second shots, or even thirds, tipping in the rebounds of his misses. One thing he couldn't seem to do was wear her down. She was in just terrific shape, and Duncan started to believe he'd have to take a time-out — maybe just a twenty-second job — before she needed to. He hadn't done much exercise for . . . well, three weeks and more; after thirty minutes, nonstop, he was sucking wind.

She had the ball, left side of the key, faked right, then switched and started to her left. He went with her, trying to force her farther from the hoop. She turned her back; he guessed she would reverse on him again: pivot, roll on back with the right-hand dribble, getting her left foot ahead of his, and spinning off his body. He took a quick step to his left, to block her.

If she'd kept on going in her original direction, she would have had an easy left-hand lay-up, but Duncan had guessed right: She wanted the reverse. So when she made her move, he wasn't where she'd planned for him to be, and instead of stepping out ahead of him, she tromped right on his instep.

The move she'd made was quick, decisive, and she couldn't stop. Her ankle turned, she lost her balance, the ball went flying toward, but nowhere near the basket, with her body (sort of) after it, and out of her control.

JULIAN F. THOMPSON

Duncan, seeing what had happened, grabbed her, just instinctively, hoping he could hold her up, help her to avoid a tumble. It didn't work. She was too big, and going much too hard. He had his hands around her lower ribs, holding on for dear life (as the saying goes). They spun, and he, a modern Sir Walter Raleigh if there ever was one, got his body under hers so when they fell he hit the blacktop on his back, and she came down on top of him.

Luckily, he'd kept his T-shirt on; they hadn't shot for "skins" or "shirts" before this game began. But still it was a fall, a pretty heavy one — perhaps a seven on the Richter scale.

He didn't hit his head, and so he couldn't claim concussion or an altered consciousness, in retrospect. No, the explanation for what happened next was that he wanted to. And so, it seemed, did she. It's even possible she started it.

In any case, they kissed.

Duncan thought he remembered the incident this way: Lying on his back, he'd looked up right into the face of what was definitely the most gorgeous gamer that he'd ever seen — a girl who in thirty intimate minutes had shown that she could play, and *loved* to play, as hard as he did. He felt so close to her, so much at one with her (one on one *is* one, after all) that kissing her was just as natural as . . . as putting up his hands on defense.

It's possible her head moved first (I mentioned this before) — that she, lying there on top of him, began the move that brought their mouths together; there was only a half a foot between them. Whatever —

once they got together, they stayed there for a while.

It would definitely be called a satisfactory kiss, from any point of view. Their mouths were like the rest of them: big and active, lean not flabby, willing to take chances, learn new moves, attempt the unexpected. They liked the taste and feel of one another, sweat and all; he changed his grip on her, and she got one hand behind his head, supporting it, the other on his shoulder. It's fair to say she also wiggled on him, slightly.

At last Caitlin Fetish picked her head up, smiled at him, and wiped her mouth on the back of her hand.

"Discontinued," she said. "Double dribble. Usually a violation, loss of possession. But not in this league. Are you okay?"

"Yeah, I think so," Duncan said. And, "Look, I'm sorry. . . . " Then he saw her roll her eyes and put a cork in it. *Overawed* is much too mild a word for Duncan. It was no more surprising that he hadn't ever met a girl like Caitlin than it was that he hadn't been fitted for dentures, say. But still.

She struggled to her feet, gimping on a tender ankle, offered him a hand, and helped to pull him up. The game was over — but, as various sages have said: It's a long season.

30. DISCOVERY

The next morning, Duncan felt pretty much the way he usually felt after the first full day of varsity basketball practice in early November, except that this time he had some deeper bruises on his back and shoulders. It'd be a few days before he could jump or rebound normally.

Caitlin, on the other hand, had iced her ankle as soon as they got back inside the house, and though it was a little achy when she first got up, at six A.M. the following morning, she would have played on it if she were being paid to, still. Falling on top of Duncan was considerably less damaging to the body than falling on a driveway was, and Caitlin reckoned that their game — from start to finish, accidents included

— had been about the most playground-type fun she'd had in quite some time.

On the walk to school that morning — book bag slung over one shoulder, maybe just the shadow of a limp — she smiled (for the fourth or fifth time since it happened) at the recollection of the final half a minute of their one-on-one. It really was — had been — a kick. She couldn't remember kissing anyone other than Lisle for a while, anyone as spontaneous, and natural, and unconniving, and big, and energetic as Duncan, for sure. She'd liked doing it; she liked *him*. It was as if she'd taken a nice refreshing sip of healthy grade-A milk, instead of her usual pony of carefully blended, expensive, and deceptively mild liqueur. That milk had satisfied, but made her kind of *thirsty*, too, she thought; she laughed out loud.

Duncan had finished painting Abraham Fetish's rooms the day before, and so had gotten on the van with Sky and Christopher and others for the trip to the health food store. It was a produce delivery day, so the van had left the house an hour earlier than usual, shortly after seven. Before that, he'd been helping with the cooking — pouring batter on the griddle, a half a ladle at a time, then flipping each round flapjack when it bubbled — and so he hadn't had the slightest chance to talk to Caitlin, not that he had anything to say.

Check that. He had lots and lots to say, all right, if nowhere near the nerve to speak the words out loud.

Standing in the shower, on the afternoon before, he'd faced the fact that he loved Caitlin Fetish. Well, not exactly *loved* (he told himself); "loved" was larger, riper, up the road. He was, however and for sure, attracted to her, very much — crazy about her, even. All he wanted was to be with her, to *play* with her . . . well, *you* know: play basketball. And fool around — whatever else might come up. The thought of touching her again, in different ways, just boggled his mind, boggled meaning "filled and thrilled" in this case. He wished she had a hundred other rooms that needed painting. As he slowly soaped his legs, he dared to hope that soon, like in a day or two, she'd find the paint she wanted (bubble-gum pink — what a great color!) and ask him to come back to work again, this time in the rooms that were her very own. Wouldn't that be something? To be around her stuff for hours at a time, and always in her space? He'd do the paint job of all time, careful and professional, for her. Lucky thing he'd had her father's rooms to practice on.

When the van arrived at the NU-HU health food complex, Duncan helped with the unloading of the produce truck. The order was a big one, so Sky stayed off the concrete platform while Christopher-the-Careful used his clipboard, thick with order forms and invoices, checking one against the other in his best storekeeper's style. When all the stuff had been piled up, he noticed Duncan standing near and doing nothing, for the moment. Christopher was not a friend of idle hands.

"Oh, Dunc," he said, "old friend. A favor, if you've got a mo'? The herb and spice shelf near the front? A lot of jars are getting close to empty. Makes the whole shelf look a little famine-ish." He chuckled. "Suppose that you could make a trip or two to B and fill up all the ones that seem to need it? Any one that's less than halfway full, at least. You know where the herbs and stuff hang out, don't you? That room in warehouse B?"

Duncan said he did, although he wasn't altogether sure. Caitlin, days before, had taken him all through that warehouse and the other, and showed him all he had to know about. He'd paid attention to the different rooms, but not complete attention. But what the hell (he figured now), he'd find the right one soon enough, by trial and error. Or he would ask someone over there. He'd forgotten that the warehouse workers, not having to unload fresh produce trucks, did not come in till nine.

In order to open the big door at the end of the huge building, he had to set down his trayful of mostly empty jars, each with its neat, hand-printed label (Bay, Cinnamon, Cloves, Cumin). Once he and Sky were inside, he remembered that there wasn't anybody there: The place *felt* empty.

"We'll just try doors," he said to Sky. "You take that side, I'll take this. Bark if you find it." Sky wagged his tail and followed Duncan.

There was a huge center aisle in the warehouse, big enough to drive an eighteen-wheeler down, but floor-to-ceiling walls had been put up on either side of it. The walls were broken, periodically, by doors, some of them of the ordinary wooden room-variety, others like garage doors that slid up. Duncan remembered Caitlin telling him, and occasionally showing him, that different products were stored, and in some cases mixed and bottled, in these different sections of the warehouse. The mixing and processing rooms, she'd said, were restricted areas — only entered by specific workers, wearing specific sanitary clothing. They were always kept locked, and even she'd never been in some of them; her father was the biochemist in the family, she'd said. As Duncan recalled, these special rooms were all in a row either on the right- or the left-hand side of the main aisle, but he couldn't remember which.

He started down the right-hand side. The first three doors were locked. I'll try one more, he thought. The fourth one should have been, but wasn't. The space he entered had no windows and was almost dark; he felt for, found, a light switch, flipped it on. Even as he did so, he was thinking: Uh-oh. Oops. Brother to one side, this Duncan wasn't brought up in a cloister; he knew what ganja smelled like in a sandwich baggie. He'd never smelled a roomful of the stuff before, however.

"Roomful" isn't fair, exactly. First of all, the room was just enormous, bigger than a lot of houses (also higher), and the section nearest to the door that he'd come in by was where the processing and packaging took place. The bales of dope that gave the place its . . . *atmosphere* were way down at the other end, stacked up near the walls, looking much like what the farmers stack for Elsie, Blossom, and the girls to spend their winters munching on. Duncan didn't start to count them; there had to be five hundred of the things, as least. What he did do was back on out of there, switching off the light in transit. Sky was in the center aisle already, looking up at Duncan with a question in his eyes, it seemed. Duncan noticed that the door had two little buttons set in its edge, just below the latch. He pressed the lower one and when he closed the door behind him, it was locked.

He went across the hall and opened doors until he found the herbs and spices room. Then he filled his jars and took them back, returning with four more. He finished replenishing all the jars before the warehouse workers came. He didn't even want to see who went in where, to work.

As far as Christopher or anyone else — except, maybe, Sky — could tell, Duncan Banigan went through his hours on the job as usual. In basketball, he'd learned to handle his emotions, hide them from opponents and the referees, his teammates, even. He played intently, evenly — working hard, but staying cool, unflustered. And so he did that day. Only Sky, with different sensory equipment (than referees or power forwards — even health food clerks) could tell that there was something wrong with him.

Duncan knew his mind was mired in an old, familiar swamp — a place he'd halfway gotten out of, so he'd thought: the land of Nothing Really Works.

It (really) was exactly everywhere, he told himself; he should have realized that. Everything's the same, including people. *Appearances* may differ, but that's all. He'd written that to Terry, just before he left: that people were probably equally rotten everywhere, or something like that. But at the time he'd written it, he'd been hoping that it wasn't so, that things'd be different in this new place, in a different state, so many miles from where he'd always been before.

And it really *had* seemed different, up until that morning. All the people were so nice, so friendly — so clean and good and purposeful, so eager to share the useful knowledge that they had, so anxious to create, contribute to, a better world. And now he'd found that part of that was cover-up, disguise.

The question was: How much? Not that it really mattered. The whole operation was contaminated, as far as he was concerned. Health food — sure. It was sort of like finding out that the Friends of the Earth or the Sierra Club owned a whole bunch of oil rigs, drilling away off the coast of Nova Scotia, just for instance.

But even as Duncan was doing all this raving in his head (while calmly continuing to wait on customers, replenish bins of beans, and wrestle sixty-pound honey cans into place on pouring racks), he knew that he was not about to up and quit the job and leave the town. The thing was: He didn't have any place to go, except back home, and he didn't want to do that.

But if you believe *that* was his main reason for deciding to stay in Burlington, Vermont, you probably should start another book.

31. ENTR'ACTES

It was hard — even dangerous — to chop vegetables and think at the same time. Duncan reached that conclusion while adding a tiny sliver of forefingernail to the pile of parsley on the cutting board in front of him. He'd then had to stop (both chopping and thinking) and search for the darned thing.

A bearded guy named Justin, working just across the board from him, had asked him what was going on, and Duncan, having found the little needle of inedible protein or whatever it was, showed him what had happened.

Justin yo-ho-hoed. "Reminds me of the time," he said, "when I was slicing onions for a specifically *vegetarian* vegetable soup. But straight into the kettle, not on a board like this. Well, I'm rapping away with Linda all the time I'm doing that, not paying a whole lot of attention to technique, so before you know it I've taken this little chunk out of my thumb, and I'm bleeding right into the soup. Here, you can still see the scar." He offered one big paw across the table, as if Duncan were a palmist. Sure enough, there was a white scar on the inside of the thumb, below the knuckle.

"Turned out the cut wasn't all that bad," he went on, "but the same couldn't be said for my ethical dilemma. It was sort of like that Campbell's commercial — the chunky one? Was my fine kettle of edibles still a vegetarian soup — or had it become a carnivore's meal? Did I have to toss the whole thing out and start over again, or what?"

Duncan shook his head: uncertain, mildly sympathetic; these folks *were* strange. "What'd you decide?" he asked.

Justin laughed some more. It seemed that almost every thought that crossed his mind amused him.

"What I decided was that seeing I was a vegetarian myself, it didn't really matter," he said. "After all, even veggies suck a cut, and anyway, I couldn't quite see myself as either meat or poultry. Even if I am a stud who's chicken of heights."

Duncan smiled, and Justin laughed so hard he started coughing.

"So what if there are ten or fifteen ignorant cannibals walking around loose in northern Vermont?" he gasped. "Part of the local color, as far as I'm concerned."

Duncan smiled some more and shook his head again. The that's-a-good-one shake. He supposed Justin was telling the truth. In any event, the story jarred his mind away from thoughts of Caitlin (What could kissing him have meant to her? Could he ask her that, directly?) and onto thoughts concerning marijuana. Did its presence in the NU-HU warehouse mean that there were other, much more dangerous (and expensive) drugs around? Or might that room that he'd unluckily discovered be just a tiny drop of blood in an otherwise estimable soup? Why, wasn't it perfectly possible that *this* pot was destined for the *legal* use of glaucoma sufferers and chemotherapy patients — whose nausea it was great for, he had read? Come on — that *could* be it, he told himself.

With that, he nodded, reached for the scallions, and tried to become one with the work, as vivacious Mona had suggested to him a few days before. At the time, she'd been wearing an orange T-shirt with a picture of a carrot recumbent on her left breast, and the words DIG IT, just below. He found that, as he chopped away at the scallions, it was, in fact, a cinch to have warm thoughts about root vegetables. ("Maniac," he told himself. "You're just too much, you know that?")

During supper, a little later on, Duncan had plenty of time to notice that Caitlin wasn't there. Her absence was not unprecedented, however. He guessed she was out with Lisle, most likely — and that got him into thinking how completely *un*likely it was that she would ever have anything further to do with him — Duncan — along the lines of . . . well, kissing and stuff like that. She *had* a boyfriend, an incredibly clean, blond doctor-type of guy who would soon be making a hundred grand a year and flying his own Lear jet. Surgeons skied, and flew their own planes a lot, he'd always heard; *he* couldn't do either of those things and probably never would be able to. Let's see (thought Duncan): Lisle'd probably fly down to Galveston, Texas, or out to Butte, Montana, where he'd save the life of an adorable little six-year-old girl by performing an operation that no one else in the world could do. *The Hardaway Procedure*, they would call it.

What chance (he further wondered) would a tall, clumsy wimpoid going into his senior year at Queen of Peace High School (Eng 4, A.P. Chem, ME Hist, Span 4, Theol 4, Soc Elec, PE) have against that kind of glamor? *The Banigan Procedures:* transplanting lots of Snickers bars from candy case to mouth; the surgical removal of a zit.

"Hey, Duncaroo," said bearded Justin, once again across a table from the lad, this time with a forkful of *tabouleh*, headed for his mouth. "You up for volleyball tonight?" A lot of Friends went in for that, out on the broad back lawn, after Clean-up.

"No, thanks," said Duncan. "Hurt my back a little yesterday. Nothing major, but it's still a pain to jump."

Though that was true enough, he also had a different after-supper plan in place: to go somewhere where he could be alone (except for maybe Sky) and think some more. That seemed important. He'd even *scheme*, conceivably. If Christopher played volleyball

— he often did — their room could be that "some-where."

Caitlin Fetish hadn't dined with Lisle that night. She hadn't really dined at all. Not that what she usually did was "dining," either. Her portions were too large, her glass of milk too tall and childish. But in this case it had simply been one of those days when she'd been on the run from pretty much seven A.M. on. Unlike a lot of people, though, she didn't feel resentment when she had a day or two like that; as a matter of actual fact, she rather liked them.

She'd gone from school to work as usual, and had spent the afternoon adrift on business correspondence (orders for the month were almost out of control). When she could see the surface of her desk again, near six P.M., she helped herself to a bag of trail mix, two tiger's milk bars, an apple, and a large papaya juice. With these, she headed back to the university library, where she planned to organize some notes and tinker with a paper she had started.

It was while she was involved in the latter activity that Caitlin found her thoughts sliding back to Duncan. The paper had to do with what medical people have chosen to call Type A males — the competitive, aggressive, achievement-oriented men who are most prone to heart attacks in middle life. Like others before her, Caitlin was wondering whether they might not be identified when they were kids, and their behaviors and attitudes modified, at least to the point that they stopped killing themselves.

Pretty soon, she started to puzzle over why some

suburban kids were able to keep life in perspective as far as competition and acquisition and aggression were concerned and others weren't. Duncan, for example, was obviously self-reliant, and an excellent competitor. He definitely would be called process-oriented rather than product-centered, she'd say — more interested in the job itself than in what he'd get out of it. He was simple and enthusiastic, but he was also mature, and a little cynical (so he seemed to claim, at least) about human nature. She bet he'd always be that way: hopeful but realistic, informed but full of wonder.

Caitlin Fetish had to smile. She was describing Duncan to herself in terms she often used *about* herself. Such a lot of jargon. The fact was that she liked his style, his hands, that kiss; none of those things had much to do with Type A, or the suburbs, or sixteen or twenty-five or any other number. No, age didn't have a thing to do with their relationship, it seemed to Caitlin Fetish. Playmates — they can be a lot of different ages. And how they get to be the way they are is totally irrelevant. The game's the thing. Or what was it that Henry Miller had written about play? "The wonderful world of play — Yes!" Something like that.

Here and now, thought Caitlin Fetish, sometime Gestalt psychologist, as she rose and closed her notebook.

There was no question about drugs being a part of this society (Duncan thought, rather grandly, to himself, lying on his back on his bed, hands clasped behind his neck, and Sky curled up near his feet). Christopher *was* playing volleyball, and so he had this room to think in, to get some things thought out, decided on. For sure.

Yes, drugs had gotten to be a part of the society, like it or not, and his own brother had been involved with them — just in a business way, of course — and in his case the involvement had killed him.

No, that wasn't right (said Duncan to himself) — *people* had killed his brother, not drugs.

He blinked rapidly, four or five times.

Stop being ridiculous, he told himself — you're meant to be thinking, not making up slogans, or being the NRA. If Brian hadn't been in the drug business, people — certain sorts of people — never would have heard of him, much less put explosives in his car. And he might as well admit that he never had believed, deep down, that what had happened maybe was an accident. Face it, Brian and his mother had been murdered. Probably because of some version of what they always put in the papers: "a drug deal that went sour." What it all added up to was that drugs could be fatal, even if you didn't take them. That was a conclusion.

He crossed his feet. There was one thing decided. He was all clear about that, rationalizations and everything to one side. Shit, he'd *always* known that, deep inside. And there was something deeply satisfying about having a position on the subject, once and for all. "An unfakeable moral position," as Brother Alphonse might say.

But the thing was (he went on thinking), he'd loved

Brian anyway, a lot. You could love somebody even if you didn't agree with what they were doing. Love was like that — a *transcendent* emotion. He wondered if that was an original thought, or from theology class at school. Either way.

Of course at this point he didn't even know if Caitlin had *any* idea about the drug part of the NU-HU operation. That's assuming — just for the sake of argument — that the drugs he'd seen *were* illegal, rather than for glaucoma or chemotherapy patients. She'd said her father was the biochemist in the family, hadn't she?

But on the other hand (Duncan had to admit) *she* was the executive vice-president, and as such would have to know (he guessed) which parts of the business were making money, and if so how much, and stuff like that. You'd have to sell two whole warehouses full of brown rice, he bet, to make as much as you would off just the amount of dope he'd seen.

No, if a person wasn't trying to kid himself, he'd have to say that Caitlin Fetish knew that NU-HU was a dealer. And if the same person happened to be in a love relationship with Caitlin Fetish, it would be his duty — an almost sacred duty — to talk her out of this involvement with the drug business before it killed her. Especially if such a person had just stood by and done nothing in another case, instead of taking any action. And had seen the tragic consequences.

Duncan grunted; Sky looked up, then put his head back down. The grunt, apparently, was not a call to action.

It was, in fact, a sound brought on by a decision and a realization. The decision was that, come what may and at the very first opportunity, he would confront Caitlin with this knowledge that he had: his awareness of the secrets of warehouse B. He would make her see how dangerous and stupid it was for her to have anything to do with that.

The realization was that his being able to love Caitlin, even if she were queen-pin of Amalgamated Drugs International, didn't amount to a hill of beans. If she didn't love *him* (which of course she didn't), there wasn't any relationship between them, which was the only thing that would make whatever he said to her meaningful, anyway. And the chances of her *ever* loving him (once he'd made this moralistic, realistic speech to her) were slim and none, respectively.

Life simply didn't work the way a person wanted it to, ever. (And now he made another sound, a sigh.) *Nothing* really worked. You get some flashes, moments, like their game the day before, or parts of it, but that's all they are. Flashes, moments, rushes. Sort of like the effects of a drug, in a way. Maybe (he thought, rather grandly — and confusedly — again) drugs copied life; their ups and downs were like a metaphor. The big game, followed by the big nothing. You can't stay up there, not for very long. Whether it was always that way (like that original sin theory seemed to say), or a recent development (as the Friends thought) didn't really matter. Either way, the same result.

There was a kind of scratching at his door.

"Yes?" responded Duncan. It wasn't in him to pretend he wasn't there. "Come on in, it isn't locked."

Caitlin smiled to see him lying there. She had a bottle in her hand. That stuff she'd shown him at the health food store, he thought. The rubbing stuff.

"I looked for you down at the V-ball game," she said, "and someone said you'd hurt your back. I feel responsible. How 'bout you come on down and let me make it better?"

She reached forward and patted Sky, who immediately rolled over on his back so she could give him a stomach scratch. As long a one as she wanted.

Duncan swung his legs down off the bed.

"Sure," he said. His mouth was a little dry. "That's really nice of you."

He followed her out of the room and down the stairs to the second floor. Drugs had, for the moment, left his mind.

160

32. RUB-A-DUB

Caitlin Fetish had a large bed, possibly a queen size; Duncan wasn't sure. He'd noticed the bed the first time he'd ever seen her room, of course, and wondered about it. In his experience, people's *parents* had double beds; he had never heard of anyone who lived in the same house as his parents having a double bed. He had especially never heard of anyone living in the same house as *her* parents having a double bed. Possibly (he told himself) she was a tosser and a turner and a sprawler: the sort of person who liked to throw her arms and legs around a lot while she was sleeping. After all, she was real tall, and huge in terms of wingspan, leg span; and when she was a pro, she surely slept in motels lots, where all the beds were doubles. A person could get used to that. A long-legged, free-spirited, athletic, easy-going, gorgeous person with a long, honey-colored braid right down to her you-know-what. The same person who was now pulling back the covers from the very bed that started all this thinking.

"Voilà," she said. "Prepare yourself for action in the miracle department. Between this magical elixir here and the skills of your humble and obedient Secretary of the Exterior, you'll think you've had a body transplant."

Duncan crossed his arms and shifted weight, feeling the way he did at player introductions before a major game. His easy grin got stiff and painful on his face, and so he licked his lips, looked down. He almost clapped his hands.

Hey, what the heck — a little rubdown scene? The lady's bedroom, on this quarter-acre bed, why not? Why sure. You tell 'em, Ben — I do it all the time.

He tried to think. His shirt. Should he take his shirt off now? He supposed so; she planned to put that glop on him, not so? He pulled the T-shirt off his head and gave it a super-casual toss onto the floor; somehow it didn't seem right to put *his* stuff on *her* chair. Especially some old gray T-shirt. *She* had a shirt that she kept on, loose, long-sleeved, and shirttail out, a real light purple; also cotton trousers, white and long, not tight, more Japanese-y than, like, painter's jeans. Minus the T-shirt, he had only the standard green running shorts plus underwear in place; he flopped down on the bed.

"Oh, wow," said Olaf the Original. The bed

smelled . . . well, delicious: a light, clean, flower-spicy, Caitlin Fetish sort of smell. He thought to add, "That's comfortable," by way of explanation.

The bed rocked slightly and he felt her straddle him, and kind of settle on his body, seat to seat.

"Here," she said, and moved his right arm so that it lay beside his head, its elbow bent. "You've got to be the bottle-holder, too." She put it down between his fingers, and he grasped it.

She rubbed her hands together, warming up the lotion she had poured in one cupped palm, and then she leaned and started in to rub his aching back.

Duncan had had backrubs in his life, before. His mother'd given him a few, when he had had to spend the day in bed, like with a real bad cold, or German measles. More recently, he'd gotten rubbed by Terry (and a girl named Ronnie, at the shore, one time), as prelude to some other kinds of touching. But he'd never before been rubbed by a pro — or if not a pro (at least at that), by a really gifted, practiced amateur.

Caitlin started with his neck, it and the trapezius muscles, which are on the tops of the shoulders at the base of the neck, and are the places that get tense and tight before exams, an interview, an argument, the kids get home from school, or any major moments in your life involving gorgeous others. After staying on them a good long while, she let her hands go sliding to his shoulders' ends, the deltoids, and quickly down the arms: both biceps, triceps, elbows, forearms, wrists. From them, relotioned, she got back to his back, this time on his shoulder blades and down below them to his waist; her strong, spread fingers made great circles on the right side of his back and then the left, probing here and gently lifting there, but never losing contact with his body, always with a smooth and slidey confidence, without the slightest hesitation. He felt as if he were a shark, perhaps a snake — in any case, some graceful, muscled creature moving through this friendly element, her hands. She varied larger motions with some smaller, more specific ones, like when she used her thumbs beside his spinal column, climbing step by step, then slipping slowly down again. The lotion had a faintly petaled fragrance, and it seemed to penetrate his skin and soothe the places that had hurt before. It warmed inside, but didn't burn the skin; he thought he felt annointed, purified — then barely could believe he'd thought that. What did he know, from "annointed"?

At different times, he almost made some sounds. They would have been (he vaguely realized) the sorts of sounds that Sky would sometimes make when he was getting rubbed. *Animal* sounds. Excusable from Sky, perhaps, but coming from a person: gross. He concentrated, kept the noise inside his head. Sky was lying on a rug beside the door. If Duncan had made sounds it would have been all right with him; he never would have laughed, or made a face, or joked about it later. He liked to have his guy enjoy himself.

Time took a walk; Duncan actually stopped thinking for a little while, and got to be just body-being-rubbed — the gentle, caring cadence of her hands. When he came back from that, he heard her humming.

Finally she stopped and tapped him on the shoulder.

"That's all you get fo' dolla, sir," she said to him. "The ma-susie's tuckered out. Of course a gentleman might offer to reciprocate, and if he did, she might revive and come back for an encore, if he liked. You like, Dunca-san?" He felt her weight come off him; the places where her thighs had straddled his were warm.

"Well," he said, a little woozily, "I'll tell you. That absolutely was the greatest backrub that I've ever had."

He got his legs around and sat on the edge of the bed. She looked at him with eyebrows raised; he shook his head and laughed.

"You were right," he said. "It was just as good as you said it'd be. That was an unbelievable feeling. I could never give you one that good. I'll try but . . . well, *you* know. I've never actually done it before, and I'd probably have to practice years before I. . . ." He heard all that ridiculous babble, and blamed it on the rub.

"Whoa," she interrupted. "You sure know how to flatter a girl. But I'll take my chances on you, rook. You look as if you've got potential."

And before Duncan had even begun to speculate on matters of mechanics, costume, tact, modesty, and so forth, she'd pulled her loose, long-sleeved lavender shirt over her head, sailed it onto a nearby chaise, and collapsed face downward on the bed. It didn't seem to matter to her that he'd been looking right at her when she started to do that, which meant that he couldn't help but get a glimpse of her small, pink-tipped breasts before they flattened on the sheet.

So there she was, naked to the waist and waiting. She pulled up her braid and tossed it to one side, out of the way. Below the drawstring white pants, she was barefoot.

Duncan guessed he just should get aboard her and begin. He took step one and settled lightly on her rear. Keeping that position might get painful; so his knees informed him, right away.

"You can put your weight on me," she said. "But you forgot the stuff." Without moving her head, which was half buried in the pillow, she pointed to the bottle on the bedside table.

When Duncan was back in position — she put her own bottle-holding hand in place — he started just as she had, on her neck and on the tops of her shoulders, making himself go slowly, gently. Although the whole idea of touching her excited him, he mostly tried to feel what she was feeling, make it be the best for her he could.

She began to make some sounds almost at once. Sky might have smiled, but Duncan, off his guard, misunderstood and stopped a second, scared that he was hurting her. But then he recognized the sounds — matched them with the ones he hadn't made, a little while before. They really didn't sound so bad, and pretty soon they put him in a sort of trance; he rocked on her a little, he wanted to bend over, kiss her smooth and shiny back, or maybe lick it. Even take a nibble — bad! — and grab her. . . . But he didn't, just kept rubbing, and time passed.

Finally Caitlin, from a point way far away, was drawn back by his voice.

"Is this okay?" his voice was asking. "I mean, shall I just keep on going. . .?"

Duncan knew that it *was* okay, when he asked those questions. But the trouble was that he'd been rubbing her for about a quarter of an hour anyway, and *his* back was starting to ache again and he figured that maybe if he asked her something he would bring her back to consciousness, and she would say, "My goodness me, that's great, it's your turn now, again . . ." et cetera.

Instead, she made a noise like "brufff." And then, "S'wonnerful. Yuhs — keepongoin', awright?"

Well, thought Duncan, if she's enjoying it all *that* much, another five minutes won't kill me.

But then he learned that she meant more than minutes — time — when she'd said "keep on going." Her body moved, her hand got underneath it at the waist and gave a tug. Then, reappearing, that same hand grabbed hold the waistband of her pants; she lifted up her hips and shoved them down, to more or less midthigh.

Duncan swallowed, stared, and then (of course) kept going. His back pain disappeared. He took more lotion, rubbed it onto both his hands and then — Eureka! — on her bottom. Aside from all the other thoughts, he thought: This can't be happening to me.

But yet, of course, it was, and when he'd finished a

most careful, dare-ful session with that part of her (at least five minutes' worth), he even dared to keep on going further, down along her thighs, pushing pants and underpants before him in a bunch. As he did *that*, she lifted up her feet: an obvious suggestion. He pulled, and there she was, the whole six feet (almost) of her, without concealment or adornment. And if that wasn't beautiful and unbelievable enough, in the next moment she'd rolled over on her back, looked at him — now very wide awake, it seemed — and smiled.

And then she raised and stretched her arms.

When she was younger, such a gesture meant she wanted to be lifted up. That was years ago, however, and Duncan, younger though he was, and semi-innocent, was not the least mixed up about her meaning. Did you ever see one of those desert movies, where someone's lost out there for days, and finally makes it to a water hole, at an oasis? Remember how that person throws himself, face forward, into it?

Well, so went Duncan, and so they had their second kiss. Familiar, it was even better, hungrier, you might say. Duncan felt so, surely.

Then he felt familiar fingers on his shorts again.

"You sure this is a foul?" she asked.

She pulled. There certainly was contact, and it seemed to be deliberate — but certainly not flagrant. He even helped; the job was somewhat harder than it was the day before.

"A foul?" she asked, and giggled, when they'd gotten him de-briefed, as well.

He searched his brain — now seething like a lava mass — for something cool to say.

"I didn't hear a whistle," he admitted.

So she laughed aloud again and naturally she whistled.

Sky, a dog of great discretion, pretended to be napping.

33. POST COITUM . . .

After Duncan left her, Caitlin Fetish just felt good. She ran hot water in the bathtub and lay in it awhile, and mused about her body, thankfully. And Duncan, necessarily. A girl friend once had asked if she had a type, "like, tall or blue eyes, rich, athletic." And she'd said "good," and the girl had nodded, laughed, thinking "good" meant skillful, knowledgeable, smooth — like, good in bed. Caitlin hadn't bothered to correct her, or add "truthful," which only was a part of "good" in any case. She felt that men learned lying earlier than women, or practiced it much harder from an early age. So much so that many men had made a whole false person out of lies, and never were their inner (truthful) selves at all. Of course she'd met some women who, she thought, had done the same. For the same sad, hopeful reasons, probably. Caitlin Fetish didn't think of *herself* as good — or bad, either. But years before, some girls in her grade school class had called her goody-goody and she hadn't liked that, which was one reason she let her friend think good-in-bed, when she'd said "good."

In any case, she knew that Duncan (who *was* good) loved her differently than she loved him: sixteen and twenty-five were different places, after all. But that was just the way it was, and love of any sort was valuable. Of course the chances were things wouldn't stay like that forever; at some point there would probably be pain. But sadness-pain — a great deal different than regret. She didn't think either of them would ever have that gosh-I-really-wish-we'd-never feeling. Goodness didn't get regretted, she believed; it made for memories a person smiled about.

Sky and Duncan tiptoed into bed without waking Christopher. Sky was happy, mellow, ready for uninterrupted sleep; looking at the guy, you'd almost have to say that he was smiling. Duncan, too; but because he'd absorbed more practical facts about anatomy, physiology, and even birth control than in the entire rest of his life up until that day, he couldn't stop playing those facts back through his mind with both amazement and appreciation.

Caitlin Fetish — now also Women with a capital W — was far more incredible and important and (yes) Wonderful than he'd ever been able to imagine anyone being, based on his previous experience and research (like what he'd heard, from such as Ben). Not that Terry wasn't a terrific girl, or anything. *Women* had an *attitude* that seemed so different from a guy's (his own), and made him feel the same. Or *let* him feel the same, perhaps — like, everything's okay and good and not-to-worry; whatever happens, happens, and the game's the thing. It popped into his mind that knowing Caitlin kind of explained certain things about Terry. Where she was coming from, what mattered to her — stuff she hadn't ever tried to tell him. Yet. Probably yet. Who could possibly know?

But Caitlin . . . he adored her. He knew about her. And he knew that she loved him, just the way he loved her. She *had* to; that was pretty obvious, like . . . *proved*. He felt well loved. Of course he did. One way or another, things would work out. It didn't matter that he'd completely forgotten to talk to her about the bales of dope in the warehouse. He'd talk to her about that in the morning — or more likely in the afternoon, when she came down to work and they could go into her office and shut the door and have a little privacy. This — what had happened tonight — would only make it — everything — work out much easier.

Love was just amazing, just amazing.

34. . . . UPS AND DOWNS

As one of those whose job was Cook-up, that next morning, Duncan spent some concentrated minutes trying to pour a perfect heart-shaped pancake on the griddle. And quite a few more trying to pour an *approximately* heart-shaped pancake. His best efforts looked more like fat, inverted tear drops, to him. But not to everyone.

"How about a stack of them-there tadpoles?" Justin asked, guffawing.

Finally, Duncan went and got a paring knife and trimmed down three ordinary round ones, just before he went off duty. By then, Caitlin had already left the dining room, so he sat and did the butter-syrup business for himself.

"Eat your heart out," a bearded, passing Bertram chuckled down at him.

Duncan laughed right back, feeling neither rancor nor embarrassment. Bert really was a card; terrific sense of humor. Everything was fun, or funny. He sang in the van, going over to work at the NU-HU store, which might have caused Christopher to ask him if he'd been in the glee club at his former school ("perchance").

When Duncan shook his head and kept on singing, Christopher then asked if he happened to know what the word *glee* meant anyway, and added, speaking louder, that he bet he didn't.

"Bet I do," said Duncan. "Happiness. And it just happens that I'm feeling happy. So pay up."

"Well, actually," Christopher said, "in the glee club sense of the word, a *glee* means an unaccompanied song, more or less like a madrigal, sung by more than two people. Which means *I* win the bet. But how come you're so happy, anyway?" He rushed to get the question in, before the music started up again.

"No reason," Duncan said cagily. "Don't you get up in the morning, sometimes, and just feel great?"

Christopher looked pleased, and took his time in answering.

"Well," he finally said, "I'm not sure. It's tempting to say, 'No, never,' but on the other hand the truth might be, 'Why, yes — I *always* do.' Adelle Davis says that if you have a hot milk drink before bedtime, and two or three calcium tablets, you ought to go to sleep easily and wake up refreshed. *I* do both those things, so I guess what I feel *is* the thing that you call 'feeling great,' which is actually a pretty inexact term and" —

Christopher flashed his upper-toothy smile — "no reason for a concert." They were almost there, by then.

So Duncan wrapped his arms around Christopher's thin shoulders and sang, at the top of his voice:

> *"Feelin' fine, feelin' great.*
> *Oh, it must have been something I ate. . . ."*

Which made the other Friends in the van laugh, and Christopher say, "Now *really*, Duncan. . . ."

All morning, and into the afternoon, Duncan tried to bite down a bit on his feelings, so as not to act outrageously excited and blissed-out. What he did was pat the dog a lot and babble on to *him*.

"Look," he said (for instance), as he unpacked paperbacks to put them in the wire racks beside the checkout counter. "It's *The Sensual Vegetarian*." He bent and showed the book to Sky. "What's that you say? A contradiction in terms? Chilly without *carne*? Hey, that's pretty good." And he chuckled and scratched the guy behind his ears, and Sky thumped his tail on the floor.

Duncan didn't think he'd ever looked forward to anything as much as he looked forward to seeing Caitlin. The feeling absolutely filled his chest and made him take deep breaths a lot, and off and on he could actually feel his heart pounding. He also felt incredibly strong and energetic, explosively so;

rather than racking books and magazines, he'd have much preferred some heavier work — like cleaning out the Augean stables, or going one-on-one with the Nemean lion, to give you two nice, classical for-instances.

As far as what was going on in the warehouse was concerned — well, he just didn't think a whole lot about that. He was pretty sure that Caitlin would be both moved and impressed by the story he would tell her. And that changes would be made, accordingly. He simply chose not to think (at all) about why she'd allowed — or perhaps even more than allowed, like *started* — this drug business to begin with. It could happen to anyone in this day and age (he thought anyway).

Then, of course, he had to say to himself — much as he hated to — that that was bullshit; dealing drugs was a choice that a person consciously made; it didn't just happen. Except if the person was an addict, maybe.

So in place of the previous thought he substituted just a touch of Scripture: "Judge not, that you be not judged."

That made him charge himself with phony piety, to which he pleaded guilty. Well. . . .

Better (he decided) to go back to thinking of her long, bare legs, and how they'd wrapped themselves around him just before he took off, soaring, into/on through/past Elysium. Oh, yes. Just classical.

When she didn't appear in the afternoon, he got a little grouchy. Time became real stubborn, dragged its feet. It was true she didn't always come to work, but still. . . .

He was waiting by the van at five o'clock and got the seat behind the driver, so he could keep an eye out for her car, in case they passed in opposite directions. That would have been the pits; it didn't happen. But he didn't sing, either.

Back at the house, he went and got a magazine and settled on the red stone steps, in front, to read. Looking up when someone ambled up the walk, or drove on in the drive, was only natural, he thought.

She finally steered the T-bird in at five to six. She'd stayed late at the library; Lisle was due at quarter past to take her out to supper. Between the car and the house, she thought, she'd make up her mind about a shower. When she saw Duncan coming toward her, she knew it was deodorant or nothing.

He was, at the same time, immensely glad to see her and irrationally (he could still admit, to himself) upset. About her not going to the store at all, and being so late getting home, as well as the whole damn business with the drugs. Of course (he'd realized on the steps) that'd *have to* come up at the same time that this other incredibly glorious thing had barely (oh!) started to happen. Wasn't that just typical of how things (never) worked?

But now he tried to fix his face so that it just looked thoughtful, sexy, welcoming, mature. He had a sinking feeling that he never got past pouty.

"Caitlin! Hi! I've got to talk to you," he started. Badly.

She smiled and put both hands up on his shoulders, pecked him quickly on the mouth. The look she'd seen on him was something more than ecstasy-warmed-over (she had told herself), something closer to the ring around love's bathtub, you might say. Question: Why?

"Well, come on up," she said, and led him to the second floor and into, not the bedroom, but her study.

"What a day," she said, and flopped into a chair. "People talk in that library just the way they would in a dining hall or a saloon. Some woman finally *screamed*, and everyone shut up for a second, and she said, '*Thank* you.' That helped for about five minutes." She looked at him. "So how was your day, love? What's happening?" Perhaps it wasn't the end of the world.

"Oh, it was okay," Duncan said. He was sitting opposite her, in the matching upholstered chair, which was covered in a bold-striped chintz. He sat forward, though, not touching the back of it at all, with his feet apart and his hands hanging down between his legs. "But what I have to talk to you about is something different. First of all, I've got to tell you about my brother, Brian — "

Three minutes into that, Caitlin knew darn well where he was heading, so she stopped him in mid-sentence ("Hold it just a sec, all right?") and left him sitting there and went into her bedroom where she called up Lisle, just catching him in time, and canceled for the night. Then she flushed the toilet, came back in, and said, "Go on."

Fifteen minutes later, she was saying, "That's

impossible. It simply couldn't be; I don't believe it."
And twenty minutes later she was saying, "Look.
I can't go down there now and prove it to you.
I've got a date with Lisle. But first thing in the
morning. . . ."

She kissed him, doing quite a job of it this time,
and meaning it. Enjoying it. Gosh *darn*, she thought.

"I wish I wasn't going, but I have to," she said.
Incredibly (to her), her voice was husky. Gosh *darn*,
she thought again, and cleared her throat. "He's an
old friend, and I can't just . . . *you* know."

And she hopped on out the door.

She used a phone booth down on Church Street, a
slice of pizza in her hand.

"How it happened doesn't matter, Daddy," she was
saying, trying not to shout. "Not right now it
doesn't, anyway. The fact is that it *was* unlocked, and
so he saw the stuff and drew the obvious conclu-
sions."

She listened for a bit.

"There isn't any choice that I can see," she finally
said.

35. SUBSTITUTION

One might logically assume that the question of who might have left the door to the room unlocked *did* come up in the course of the four hours (eight to midnight, inclusive) that it took the people who ordinarily worked during the daytime in that room to load those many bales (and hundredweights) of marijuana onto the eighteen-wheeler parked in the aisle. As a matter of fact, if one were to go a step further and imagine that accusations flew back and forth for almost that entire time, along with worn-out, uncreative epithets (oh, "fuckin' moron ," "careless asshole," "stupid shit," that crowd), one would not be being fanciful at all.

And after *that* truck pulled out, and the other one

pulled in, at three A.M., the men that came with *it* were not delighted either. They also used some language that (according to my mother) showed they lacked vocabulary, taste, and I forget what else. But I doubt they'd value her opinion. Their targets, unsurprisingly, were the people whose failure to lock a door had cost a group of colleagues (in another state, yet) six hours of hard lifting, loading, and unloading, and a good night's sleep to boot.

Abraham and Caitlin Fetish supervised the entire operation, and between trucks (i.e., midnight and two forty-five) worked feverishly themselves, with dustpan, broom, and Hoover, to make sure that there were no incriminating . . . residues.

"As far as I'm concerned," she said to him when they had finished, "this is absolutely it. The End. Call it a sign, a portent, an augury — anything you want — but I get one clear message from what's happening. And that's that we get out of the consciousness-altering business as of now. Declare the subdivision closed. We definitely don't need it. Why push your luck, incredible as it is? I mean, who else in the world could start a health food business as a cover-up for a dope ring and have it turn into a major gold mine?"

Abraham Fetish made her a deep bow, with full arm gesture. He looked pleased. "A sign, you say?" he said. "You're right. 'The salt has lost its savor, the sycophant his favor, the chewing gum its flavor' — *I* said that. You know, I've kind of had the same thing on my mind for weeks. Some workers may object to taking country roads instead of Interstates, but what

JULIAN F. THOMPSON

the heck. We'll stuff them full of jujubes and ginseng root and offer to retrain them. They'll be better off in the long run. Where *are* the snows of yesteryear, I ask you. In the bottom of the deep blue sea, that's where."

Caitlin shook her head. After years of fruitless (not to mention endless) argument, it looked as if she'd finally got her way. And not because of anything she'd done or said or thought of, though — just because he (finally) agreed with her. Or something. She would *never* understand her father.

So, to get — oh, slightly — even, she looked him in the eye and said, *"N'entrez bien le fox away."*

And she headed for the shower that would have to take the place of one night's sleep.

36. SHOW AND TELL

"Look," said Caitlin Fetish. "You say you're not a doper, right?"

It was 8:15 A.M. Right after breakfast she had driven Duncan (and his faithful dog) directly to the NU-HU complex by the lake. No one else had come to work yet; soon she'd have to leave and go back up to class.

The three of them were standing in the large room in the huge warehouse, facing one great wall of bales, and two of them were sniffing — the one with much the better nose at real close range. There were bales of different herbs (still waiting to be ground, or bagged, or bottled), bales of other plants (alfalfa, trefoil, cattails, camomile), even bales of wheat and barley (not yet winnowed, on the stalk). A lot of different smells were mingled in the air.

"Well, no," said Duncan. "Or, rather, I mean *yes*, I guess I'm not. I've tried the stuff, of course — *you* know, a few hits here and there" — he meant to sound offhand and cool about it — "and to tell you the truth, it didn't do a whole lot *for* me. But still. I've seen it around ever since grade school, and I've certainly smelled it enough. People are always coming up to you and saying, 'Take a whiff of this, it's pure Tasmanian, strong as a mountain gorilla.' Stuff like that. So I'm sure I know what it smells like. At least I've always thought I did." The thing was, the room pretty much *looked* the same as it had two days before, but he didn't think it smelled the same. *Then* it had smelled more like . . . well, *dope*.

"I'm sure you do," Caitlin said. "That's *if* you're smelling something in a plastic baggie, underneath your nose. And you've already been told what it is, in the first place. I mean, don't you think it's possible that if some kid who you knew was a real head shoved a bag full of *this* in your face, and told you it was Pakistani Platinum, that you'd believe it?"

And she reached on top of a bale and took a grab of whatever it was and rolled it together in her fingers and then held them under his nose.

Of course he nodded, up and down.

"You see?" she said. "That's catnip."

"Is it?" he said. "Wow. That sure smells lots like pot to me."

And yes, it surely did (he told himself). It seemed he wasn't all that big an expert; she was right. It was also true that he hadn't spent a whole lot of time in the room, although he didn't exactly rush in and out, either. He'd been completely positive that there'd been marijuana in that room, and lots of it. Now he wasn't quite so sure. On the one hand (he told himself again) the room *looked* the same as he remembered it — but it certainly seemed to smell different. Didn't it? Or *did* it? How could he be sure?

In his mind, he still was going back and forth when Caitlin played her ace, the ultimate high card, the absolute shut-uppa-your-face: *She said that what he'd thought just couldn't be.* She said that she would have to know if NU-HU'd ever bought, or stored, or sold, some dope — if they had anything to do with dope.

"And," she said, her hand laid flat upon a bale, "I swear we don't."

"Well, then, I guess I must have been mistaken," Duncan said. He smiled and shook his head as he said it, but his face felt all wrong, and his voice sounded phony, to him.

"You don't believe me," Caitlin said. She dropped her eyes. She was wearing light blue pants and a white silk shirt, and she had a black Shetland sweater thrown over her shoulders with the sleeves loosely knotted in front. Her long braid had a piece of light blue wool tied around it, near the end.

"I *do*," Duncan said, quite a bit louder. "I really, really do." That sounded much better. He couldn't let her think that he thought she was lying to him —

or maybe didn't know what the hell was going on in her own company. What kind of a friend would that make him? What kind of a *lover*, better make that, right? My gosh, imagine (Duncan thought): *him* somebody's lover, like in the *New York Post*. Kids his age were never *lovers*, were they?

"If you say there wasn't any pot in here, that's good enough for me," he said. "Plenty good enough. I mean it. You're right. I don't know all that much about the stuff, my brother was the big authority. I'm just the sole surviving paranoid . . . *you* know." He pressed the words, the little joke, right into her.

It worked. Her eyes came up. She smiled a sad and understanding smile and reached and touched him on the cheek. Then she stepped up close and slid one arm around him, tilted up her chin. Of course he grabbed her, kissed her almost desperately — the way a lover would have surely done. Her mouth came open, wide; she pressed herself against him, and while the kiss went on, she kept on making small adjustments in position.

"Oh, *Caitlin*," Duncan said, when they had broke apart, both gulping.

"I have to go," she said. "Could you — possibly — come up, like, after work? Meet me in my study? There's something I want to show you, right next door to it." She grinned at him. "Or, if you're not up for that, we could always sit and chat."

Driving back up Shelburne Road, she shook her head a lot and, one time, hit the steering wheel a good one with her palm.

"Gosh *darn*," she said again.

Duncan had a most confusing day. Anticipation (make that "hunger for") his rendezvous with Caitlin was much (much, much) the most persistent thought/ emotion in his mind, and also body. Yes.

"Woof," he said to Sky, one time, and then again: "Arrr-*oof*!"

Sky wagged his tail and might have winked at him.

He was now (Duncan told himself between such thoughts) ninety-nine and forty-four one-hun- dredths percent sure that he had smelled no pot in that warehouse — that it had been a mild hallucina- tion, or delusion, or whatever you might want to call it, based on the still unresolved feelings that he had, going back to Brian's and his mother's deaths. That made perfectly reasonable good sense; he didn't have to think about the matter any more. It was just too bad Sky hadn't gone to one of those narcotics detec- tion schools some dogs attend, at government expense. But if he had, it probably would have changed him, certain ways. His present haircut would have been okay, but not his easygoing, very near *permissive*, nature. And he'd have had to get an attaché case, that's for sure.

In midafternoon Duncan was replenishing the fruit juices in the big refrigerator when Christopher appeared across the aisle (clipboard at the ready, natch) checking on the shelves that held the Nu-Hu teas and different sorts of soup mixes.

"Boy," said Duncan, lightly and with half a laugh,

"some of those uncaffeinated teas — the ones with the different herbs in them? — they smell more like something a person'd *smoke*, instead of put it in hot water, don't you think? You suppose anyone's tried to do that? *You* know — tried to get high on a NU-HU product, thinking it was — I don't know — like pot, or something?"

As far as Duncan could tell, looking out of the corner of his eye — and, like many good ballplayers, he had excellent peripheral vision — Christopher didn't react to that at all. He kept on writing numbers, or whatever, on his charts.

"Seven Moody Mint," he mumbled to himself. "Oh, sure," he said, now louder. "I've known people who'd try anything — *every*thing. Back on Three Mile Island? You wouldn't believe it. There was this one kid who claimed he could get off on a certain mushroom *soup*."

"Well, it crossed my mind," Duncan said, "that a place like this'd be a great set-up for selling real drugs. I mean, so much of what we stock looks just about like something else. All those vitamin pills, and different capsules we put out, as well as the dried stuff. You know what I mean?"

Christopher looked serious. "I don't think it's a good idea to even *talk* that way," he said. "I mean, even to me. There are a lot of people out there" — he made a vague, far-distant gesture with one hand — "who'd like to see the Nukismetic Humanists get in any sort of trouble. My father, just to give you one example. I think he thinks we're just one step away from being Communists, living in community, like this."

He came over close to Duncan and put a hand on his shoulder. "This place is *squeaky* clean," he said. "It has to be. We're in the business of survival, Dunc."

And he nodded once, emphatically, and turned back to his shelves.

37. CHANCE ENCOUNTER

When Duncan hit the carpeted staircase in the NU-HU house on South Willard, at 5:18 P.M., he was already flying. But Sky still passed him before he'd gotten to the first landing, halfway to the second story. Having four on the floor gives a guy an edge, when it comes to going up the stairs — not to mention flat-out speed and leaping ability.

So, what this meant was that Sky, digging in hard with his toenails as he negotiated the required U-turn, very nearly collided with a small robed figure coming down from the second floor.

"Hey, buddy — hair's on fire?" Mister Carlo hollered at him, startled. He halfway turned to watch the animal go by him, which meant he got a good long look at both the comet and its tail: the lanky boy who zoomed up three steps at a stride, only two-three yards behind the dog.

Duncan had his mind on large importances: a swift but thorough shower; should he risk a shave?; a total change of clothes. Then, one flight down to rendez-vous in . . . heaven. Of course he saw the little man, and even thought he looked familiar, vaguely. But there were lots of Friends who liked to wear that NU-HU lounging robe, and weren't tall, and had good reason to be coming down those stairs.

" 'Scuse us," puffed Duncan, much too late, of course.

He was, by the time he got the words out, already past the second floor and heading for the third, his belt unbuckled and his mind below it, if you have to know the truth. Don't forget (he told himself while entering his room) to brush your teeth, and maybe borrow just a shake or two of Chris's talc-free, scented, baby powder. . . .

38. IT'S EITHER
HIM OR ME (PART 1)

Mister Carlo, though, was much, much less distracted — in terms of having other pressing matters on his mind. He was, after all, *not* racing to a meeting with the girl — hey, make that *Woman* — of his dreams. Instead he was, in rather boring fact, proceeding toward the living room with some vague thoughts of picking up a game of Chinese Checkers with someone. Male or female, carnivore or veggie — it didn't really matter who.

Seeing Duncan wiped that plan out in a hurry.

"Oh, Lee *Christmas*," Mister Carlo muttered. Gathering his robe around his thighs, he turned and scuttled back up to the second floor, and down the hall, and once again to Fetish's calm study: newly painted blue, with rugs of gray.

"Abe!" he cried, as he burst in. It seemed that chromotherapy (as it was called in days gone by) had no effect on Ecuadoreans (if that's what Mister Carlo was). There were heebies in that syllable he cried, and jeebies in his eyes.

"He's here!" he said. "That kid is *here*. The one from down in Jersey. I just now saw him onna stairs. He's right here in this house. He's come to get me, Abe!"

Abraham Fetish had been standing in front of the big round mirror on the wall, trying to clip the hairs in his nose with the scissors from his desk. He turned, his left palm up and out, in a calming gesture, the long scissors in his right hand closed, and pointing up. He looked for all the world like a large, absentminded orchestra conductor.

"What?" he said, quite sharply. "The boy you were looking for down there, up here? Incredible. Impossible! Is this some kind of a yo-yo joke? I don't believe it."

Fetish put the scissors on his desk and paced the length of the room to the window. In the style of the late Humphrey Bogart, he pulled the curtains almost closed and peered around the edge of one of them. The lawn behind the house was empty.

"But even if the boy were here," he added, turning back toward Mister Carlo, "what makes you think he's come to get *you*? 'If the mountain comes to Mohammed, must the Prophet take up skiing?' Pantsful, 85."

Mister Carlo groaned and sank down in an easy chair. By chance, his arms both rested on the chair's; his hands were tightly clenched fists. Fans of capital punishment, noticing his posture, might have been reminded — thought about — a favorite cancer cure of theirs: electrocution. The thought that came to Mister Carlo's mind — and very much unbidden — was another one, however: *It's either him or me.*

Mister Carlo groaned again. Those five damn words. They'd been, in part, responsible for *everything*.

He'd been down there in New Jersey, his mission to take orders (so-and-so-many bales of this, or kilos of that, or caps of something else) and what's he find but someone's underselling them, across the board. This guy named Brian Banigan. Of course he'd gotten on the phone to Fetish right away — his buddy Abe, his boss. And naturally old Abe had glowed on top. Which means he starts in hollering:

"It's either him or me. You hear me, Carlo? One of us is going to have to go, that's all there is to it."

And then:

"The name's a fake, I guarantee you. It's gotta be some creep I know, from high up in another . . . company. An organization man, you get my meaning? There's only two-three outfits big enough to try to do this to me." Fetish had paused, then drawn a big, deep breath and let it out so suddenly and noisily that Mister Carlo had had to jerk the receiver away from his ear.

"Okay, then," Fetish had finally gone on. "There's

just one way for us to move on this. You listen to me good. I know this isn't something that you've done before, but you can handle it, I'm sure. First, you find this so-called Banigan. Then you go and buy the stuff you need. Get the best equipment — right? — no junk; the better stuff works better. What I want you to come back up here with, when you come, is a real clear picture of this guy, blown up. You understand? I don't care where you take him. Probably outside somewhere would be the easiest — on his porch, in his car, something like that. *You* do that, and *I* can find out which organization's behind him, all that stuff. We just can't have this kind of unnatural behavior. Why, it's contrary to the laws of physics, which plainly state that no two objects can occupy the same place at the same time. You see that, don't you, Carlo? *It's either him or me.* That simple. One of us has got to go."

And Mister Carlo had gulped and said, "You sure of what you're sayin', Abe? You're serials?"

And Fetish had given a merry little chuckle and said, "You're fuckin' A I am, my little friend. There's some things a wise man can't forgive. 'With countenance funereal, and manner magisterial, he said: Drop dead, my dear-eal; I *know* that it's venereal.' Concupiscence, 26 to 30. I'm counting on you, Carlo."

And Abe had hung it up.

Mister Carlo'd gone ahead and done it, just as Abe had told him to. It hadn't been so easy, either, getting all the stuff he had to have, and learning how to use it. But he'd done it.

When he'd blown up the car (with Brian and his mother *both* inside it — God forgive him) and taken four quick snapshots of the mess, he'd called up Fetish with the news and learned that he had made one horrible mistake. Abe had never meant for him to *kill* the guy, just take his picture — but he hadn't said it right. He absolutely hadn't. The *real* fault (Mister Carlo told himself, from time to time) was Abe's; he'd grown up in these United States and speaking English — it was up to him to talk so people understood what he was saying.

In any case, and regardless of whose fault it was, Mister Carlo had fled wildly, blindly, from the scene and state. He'd traveled down, by bus, to Baltimore, fighting off the nauseating waves of guilt that mixed with the exhaust. Once there, he'd eaten crabs (which he despised) for two whole days, before he'd come back to his senses, in a way, and had gone north again to Jersey, planning to confront the younger brother of the man he'd killed, tell him what the truth was, and promise him . . . well, anything. Abe had lots of money and a heart with lots of mush in it (with mouth to match, thought Mister Carlo). He and Abe, *both* guilty — they'd both do something for the boy.

But what had happened (as you know) was that Mister Carlo had lost his nerve in the funeral home, and hadn't talked to Duncan. Instead, he'd run away again, this time to Allentown, PA., where he ate scrapple and audited classes at Muhlenberg College for close to three weeks, even taking — just for the hell of it — a quiz in a course called the Psychology of

Social Hours (Psosh 122), on which he got an 83, better than a running back and two defensive tackles. By the time he returned to New Jersey again, Duncan was nowhere to be found.

Until just now, that is.

"Look, Carlo," Abraham Fetish said, when he didn't get an answer to his question about Mohammed and skiing. "You're still upset from everything that's happened in the last six weeks, and that means, Point Number One" — he held up a large forefinger — "it probably wasn't the same boy. So, Point Number Two" — his middle finger rose — "you just point out who you *think* it is, to me, tonight at supper. Then, Point Number Three, if I can't satisfy you as to who the person is and why he isn't who you thought it might be, well, then, we'll think of what we ought to do. All right?"

He slapped his hands together: one, two, three. "No one's going to get you. You have my word on that. There's an old French proverb that applies. DeFoigrave, I think. '*Quand le potage est quelque chaud, il ne faut pas faire le feu avec la serviette.*' Translating: 'You don't kill the waitress when the soup is cold.'"

Fetish put a gentle hand upon his friend's right shoulder. "Don't worry, Carlo — really. This whole thing is *my* fault and my responsibility. To the extent that it is anyone's, that is." He paused.

"Even a boy could see that — wherever he may be," he said, and might have shuddered.

"At least it wasn't a *nuclear* bomb," he said, trying to end the conversation on a lighter note.

39. HOT STUFF

Ordinarily, Mister Carlo would have gotten a lot of pleasure out of that night's dinner. As every stereotyping reader's probably assumed by now, this small Hispanic-looking man enjoyed hot food. One of the resident Friends, a girl from New Jersey (all of whose ancestors for the past five generations had lived in central and eastern Europe, if you must know) made a Mexican casserole of refried beans, with cheeses and tortillas, in a hot tomato sauce that . . . well that always got ol' Mister Carlo's taste buds to slip on their *huaraches* and go wild.

But this particular evening there was no way he could concentrate on his food. The man was plainly in a state, and the state was *not* Chihuahua. Indeed, his constant wiggling, his constant craning of the neck, and questions-questions-questions even made it difficult for Abraham Fetish, seated at his left, to dine with any real enthusiasm. A nice cold Bud — now *that* went well with Mexican; a jumpy little buddy didn't.

"But Carlo-*mio*," he said at one point, chewing through the first three words, then swallowing. "It is a fact that people do eat out sometimes. Just for the fun of it. It doesn't have to be a plot, that he's not here. Assuming that you're not mistaken altogether."

"Wait, wait," said Mister Carlo, staring at the kitchen door, which had only just swung shut. "I think I maybe spotted him. Just then. He's hangin' out right back there in the kitchen. You come with me, all right? It only take a second."

Fetish sighed, put down his fork and napkin, and preceded the little man into the kitchen. Carlo attached himself to the back of Fetish's right shoulder, holding onto his wrist. More or less concealed, he raised the wrist halfway to shoulder height and peered beneath the armpit of his friend before he straightened up and shook his head.

"No," he whispered. "It's not him."

"Of course not," Fetish said. "That's Charlie . . . Charlie *something*. From Toledo, I believe. But I'll give you this much: He does look just the way you said that young man looked — tall, no facial hair, et cetera. Are you sure that's not him? Positive? I bet it *was*. And Charlie here, he isn't anybody's brother from New Jersey. You can bet your life on that, right, Chazz?"

The man addressed, completely at a loss, just smiled and shrugged. Fetish laughed a hearty one; they went back to their table.

"No," said Mister Carlo, sitting down, "that's not the one I saw before. I'm pretty sure. I *know* it isn't. What happened was — I bet — that other one, he spotted me, and now he's taken off and gone an' . . . gotten into my place, and *hidden* there, like underneath the bed or in the shower, maybe. Just waitin' till I come back in and then" — he drew his pointer finger straight across his throat, from left to right, with appropriate sound effects.

"Oh, Abe," he wailed, "I don't know what I'm gonna do. He's come to get me, an' he's crazy wild. You know he'd have to be. Blood Thursday." He glanced down at his watch and nodded. The watch told him the time, the day, and date, and tried to guess his weight, sometimes.

"Look, Carlo," Fetish said in desperation. "I'll tell you what we'll do. Just let me finish my supper, and then we'll go over to your apartment together, pack a suitcase up, and. . . ."

So, within the hour, Mister Carlo was installed on the second floor of the NU-HU house, in the Fetishes' own guest room — a few steps down the hall from where fair Caitlin went to bed each night. Or even earlier, sometimes.

Caitlin Fetish wasn't one to rehash her decisions. As a general rule, she'd decide where she wanted to get to and which road she wanted to travel on, and then she'd just take off and not look back.

When she met Duncan at her study door at 5:45 P.M., she took him by the ears and kissed him. And it didn't take her more than five minutes to maneuver the two of them into the bedroom next door and out of the clean clothes that each of them had only just put on. As said before, Caitlin Fetish liked all aspects of this tall, lean, limber, muscled, gentle, honest boy. That afternoon and early evening, he grew on her some more. His modesty was never coy or sheepish, and he often laughed out loud when things felt good. He touched the same way that he talked: carefully and lovingly, but still he wasn't always in control (like someone she could name). He definitely could carry her a ways away, and if she led a lot, in what they did together, it was just because she knew the routes and destinations better.

A little after eight o'clock, Duncan (feeling maybe ten feet tall, but totally relaxed as well) was lying on his side, his cheek upon his upper arm. He'd (also) never felt so much like talking in his life. (Do I mean "babbling," perhaps? You bet.)

"Boy," he said, "I can't begin to tell you how you've made me feel. It's the most amazing thing. You know what it's like? It's like I used to be a lump of clay and then you breathed on me like you were God or something — aren't I original? — and so I got to be a person. But that's exactly what happened. All of a sudden, thanks to you, I felt the way I used to feel before, but better. Maybe fifty times as good.

"You see, the thing is" — he propped his head up on one palm — "a little while after Brian and my Mom got killed, the strangest thing seemed to happen to me. I more or less went numb. You know what I mean? I guess I still felt stuff, but on a very low level. Nothing was very good and nothing was very bad; everything was in this real narrow range. You know how skimmed milk tastes? Well, that's it. You can't say it's awful really, but it isn't *milk*." He laughed at himself. "That's what I was feeling like. Skimmed milk. And what else blah? Like boiled potatoes, maybe. Not a french-fry in the house, no kidding. Whatever people were talking about, or I was doing or thinking about, I just couldn't care less. That's mostly the reason that I came up here in the first place. Nothing mattered down there; nothing worked. I couldn't get excited about anything — school, basketball even, my so-called future, college. I don't mean to be gross, but I couldn't even get excited about my girl friend, if you know what I mean."

"I think I might," said Caitlin, cautiously. And laid her hand down on his side, between his ribs and his hip bone. She thought the conversation could be heading toward a place she'd just as soon not go to. And anyway, she liked to touch him. Anyhow.

"I didn't even particularly want to come up here," he said, "but I didn't *not* want to, either. And I knew I didn't want to stay where I was, just middling along and making everybody else feel bad. So, well, I came on up. And even that first day, when I met you outside the house — remember? — I started to feel different, much more — "

"Wait," she said. "One thing I never asked you. How come you *did* come up here, anyway? That story you told me — about being on some independent study or something — that was just made up, wasn't it? So how come you did come up here, specifically to Burlington? And how come you were standing out there on Willard Street and staring at the house?"

"Oh, yeah," he said. "Well, that's the most amazing thing. Somehow or other, my brother must have heard of the Nukismetic Humanists, and learned all about what they think and everything, because he'd written me this note, and left it in an envelope, down in. . . ."

She looked at him and thought: He really does look happy; he is beautiful. And then she got that unfamiliar twinge, the one she'd had a time or two before in the last day and a half, the one that'd made her think, Gosh darn. She didn't call it feeling guilty, but she could have. How would he look if he ever found out she'd lied to him, so carefully, so artfully? How would she like to see him then? She hadn't had a choice — no way — but still. . . .

And as he kept on talking, she got another little . . . not twinge this time, more like a blip, a warning on her radar screen. The way that he was telling it, the message from his brother said he ought to check out *Fetish* (on South Willard, Burlington), not Nukismetic Humanism. What made him think that Brian had *philosophy* in mind? Here's the way it looked to her: His brother had been dealing drugs, her father had been dealing drugs. *Ergo*: a connection.

"You know," the boy was saying, "I think I've said before I don't believe in fate, exactly. I mean the way the Friends do — right? — with their nuclear 'event,' the way they say, and all that. I mean, believing in that particular kind of fate seems too much like someone's giving up, just letting it happen, almost *helping* it to happen. By saying, 'Well, I'm just one person and what I do doesn't matter, and anyway maybe something good will come of it.' That kind of thing. But what I *was* starting to say was" — he smiled at Caitlin, reached, and very gently (she'd have said "adoringly," let's face it) touched her breast, and kept his hand there — "that it really does sort of seem as if I were *meant* to come up here, and meet you, and be with you. You know? It's such a good thing — for everyone, it seems like. I mean, you could *almost* say — " he started.

Caitlin put her hand on his, the one that touched her breast, and rolled onto her back, keeping his hand there, cupped now on her flattened breast.

"It *is* a good thing," she said, and sighed. "A wonderful thing. Wonderful things happen, and they should happen to you. Not that I'll ever believe that your mother and brother being killed connects to us in any way. That'd sound to much like Nookie-talk" — she smiled — "as Lisle would say."

Duncan shook his head, more at the sound of the word *Lisle* than anything else. He hadn't meant *that*, of course: that their dying was some sort of a prerequisite to him meeting Caitlin. All he'd wanted to say was how fantastically special their . . . affair? — no, *love relationship*; affair sounded too casual . . . how fantastically special their love relationship had been, would be.

He took the hand that had been propping up his head and put it on her bare, smooth shoulder; he leaned to kiss her on the lips. Sometimes, when they were talking — it had happened then, just then — he'd feel, well, *young* compared to her, which made him wince a little, in discomfort. But when they *did* stuff (he believed), then there weren't any ages (he moved his hands again, his head, his body), just the happenings, the feelings, the excitement.

"Real hot stuff." He said the words without intending to, his mouth now on her rib cage, sliding all around.

Caitlin smiled and tousled his hair.

40. IT'S EITHER HIM OR ME (PART 2)

   When Mister Carlo retired to his brand-new room
— the guest room on the second floor, with Fetishes
on either side of him — it still was early in the evening. He had heard the expression *a low profile* and
although he didn't understand it, quite (you put your
face down onna floor?) he got the general idea and
knew it was the kinda thing he'd give a lot to have one
of. Mister Carlo didn't want any part of his anatomy
to be visible just then, and especially not in his own
apartment in Winooski, or in any of the public rooms
in the NU-HU house. If it were, he was pretty sure it
would get shot off (or cut, or otherwise divided off)
by the brother of the man he never should have

killed, down in New Jersey. Or by the son of the woman. Either way, he'd end up looking very different, good and dead.

Now he needed just to figure out what he should do, beside the profile bit. No matter what, the phrase *It's either him or me* kept coming to his mind, as if it were some hallowed, universal truth, the thought that justifies, right up there on a par with "Well, they did it to me" (which may have kept as many small, foul practices in place as the better-known immortal "I'm just following orders"). It wouldn't be fair for the boy to kill him, because it hadn't been his idea to kill the boy's brother. *That* had been done by mistake, because of bad communication and misunderstanding. The sort of human error that wouldn't happen to two basically peaceful, easygoing guys like him and Abe but once in a couple of billion times, he'd bet. You could almost say it'd *never* happen — that particular kind of foul-up. It had maybe never happened before in all of human history, and never would again. And anyway, "Two wrongs don't have to make a fight." Wasn't there a saying like that? And if so, mightn't it apply, somehow, to this situation?

Mister Carlo wasn't sure; the whole thing was so confusing.

But back to *It's either him or me*. The thing was: He knew what both of them were thinking, what their two basic attitudes were.

The boy wanted to get him. It wasn't right, it wasn't proper, it was even what you might call evil (even though the boy himself wasn't evil). But that was the way his feelings were leading him. Following his feelings, the boy would get him if he had the chance.

He, on the other hand, didn't want to get anybody, but here was this . . . threat, this danger coming at him. What was he meant to do? Stand there? Get killed dead, or maybe mutilated anyway? Wasn't it right for him to strike while he still could, knowing what he knew? If he waited, he'd get hit, for sure; it was just a matter of time. Wouldn't it make a lot more sense to strike while he still could? *It's either him or me.*

Mister Carlo nodded. He'd have to choose a weapon, and it better be the right one. He'd brought some with him from his apartment (a knife, some rope, a hammer)—stuffed them in his bag while Abe was looking in the shower for him — and there were others in this house, he felt quite sure. He needed something like the Wild West marshals used to use — The Pacifier, wasn't it? — where they'd put one in the bad guy's mouth and he'd go straight to sleep.

But first, he told himself, he maybe should consider a disguise.

There was a light above his dresser, a mirror on the wall behind it. Mister Carlo went and stood there, stared at his reflection. Shave the mustache off? Pair a glasses, maybe? A little pada 'lectric tape in both his cheeks — make him look a little fatter?

Mister Carlo never heard the footsteps in the darkened hall — so great was his concentration on his face, his problem. But Duncan, going by, looked in (who could resist?) and saw the little man, again.

Now out of the robe he looked, if anything, a little more familiar. Some friend of Abraham's, thought Duncan, must be. Probably a big shot in the Nukismetic movement. He wondered if a guy like that believed he knew, already, both the where and when of this anticipated nuclear "event." And he wondered, once again, how any person could justify saving himself while letting other people — even any single other person — die.

Possibly he'd think: It's either him or me, thought Duncan.

41. TE-LE-PHONE

Sky hadn't made the trip to Caitlin's room with Duncan. Instead, he'd gone with Christopher to help in any way he could with that night's dinner for the Friends (including tasting parts of it, for sure). Then he'd eaten his own meal, watched a half a dozen games of volleyball, and gone back to their room to grab a wink or two. When Duncan came upstairs, and asked him if he'd like to take a walk, he was delighted. Walks were always fun, and he was pretty sure that Duncan hadn't eaten, yet. Sky wasn't what you'd call a moocher or a pig, just a normal, healthy, growing dog who'd learned while on the streets to get it when you can.

They went down to a place called the All-American Hero, and Duncan got a large roast beef and milk (wag, wag). Then they crossed the street and sat down in the park to eat and muse about such things as love, and how much Mr. Hagerty would hate the idea of Duncan's playing at UVM rather than at Notre Dame or UCLA or UNC, and whether it'd still be great when she was thirty-five and one of them was only twenty-six or seven, and the other merely twelve or so.

By the time they'd walked back up South Willard Street Duncan had forgotten all about the little man he'd seen inside the guest room on the second floor. When they reached that landing, heading up to bed, Sky had stopped and waited for a moment. Were they going visiting? he seemed to ask. But Duncan only glanced at Caitlin's bedroom door, and smiled, and kept on going to the third.

The next morning, the two of them breakfasted and left for work before — oh, long before — there was an open eye in Mister Carlo's room. Neither fear for his life nor (possibly) the need to plan and execute a clever and preventive strike were going to interfere with Mister Carlo's wish to get a good ten hours' worth of sleep. He also took (don't act surprised) a nap each midday, after lunch. Come on — you *knew* he would.

The work day at the NU-HU store was pleasant, uneventful. Duncan realized he liked what he was doing. It was a good business, a beautiful store. It was fine to be able to make healthy products available to good people. There should be even more NU-HU stores than there were, all over the country. Maybe, someday, there would be. Duncan nodded to himself, when he thought that.

Caitlin didn't ever show, but Duncan didn't worry. He had his job to do, just as she had hers. When he and Sky got vanned back home to Willard Street, he headed right upstairs and to their room, and started to undress, get ready for his shower. She'd probably be home around the time he finished. Or shortly afterwards. It didn't really matter.

"Dun-can!" A voice came floating up the stairs. The back stairs, as it happened — the ones that, years before, the servants used. His room was very near them, at the far end of the hall. The calling voice was cheerful, Justin-Roger-ish.

"Yes — what?" yelled Duncan, from his doorway.

"Te-le-phone," the voice replied. "You can take it in the hall up there — okay?"

Caitlin, Duncan guessed. Just checking in with him to let him know when she'd be coming home. How nice. He slipped his shirt back on. The phone was on a small oak table, not far from his door. He went and picked up the receiver.

"Heh-lo," he said. He sounded smooth and loud. Important.

"Duncan?" she said. "Duncan, is that you? It's Terry."

"Terry!" Duncan said. Now *very* loud, and he was smiling. Then he thought: Yikes, Gulp.

"Tare!" he said. "How *are* you?"

"I'm fine," she said. "I'm in a phone booth, with quarters up to here, so don't worry. I got the number from Directory Assistance. Dottie gave me the name of the people you're staying with. I just wanted to call."

"I'm glad you did," said Duncan. He tried to think just what it was he should be saying. *Would* be saying, normally. "How *are* you, anyway? What's going on? How's school and all? How's Ben?" That was a pretty good string of questions, he thought. His heart seemed to be pounding a lot harder than it had any reason to.

"I'm okay," she said. "Everything's okay. I miss you, though. A lot. That's the only bad part, but it's enough. I just don't like not being with you."

She sounded exactly like Terry, Duncan thought. Her voice sounded just the same as it used to, just the way it would have sounded if they'd talked two hours before. And the things she'd said sounded like her, too — direct and honest, no big melodrama, just saying whatever she was feeling.

"Yes," said Duncan. "I know what you mean." He hoped she took that right. "So how's Dottie doing? Did you talk to her lately? How about all the stuff with the cops and everything?" He was shocked to realize how much he didn't want to talk about Brian and his mother.

"Things are really almost back to normal," Terry said. "I guess they're still investigating all of it, and looking out for you. But no one comes around much any more, and Dottie and I are a whole lot less paranoid than we used to be. I swear, for a while back there it was crazy. Like we were under — what's it called? —*surveillance*, or something? One day there'd be regular police cars, parked, or driving up and down the street real slow. Then you wouldn't see any of *them*, but after a while you'd notice the same men — you know, just in regular clothes — sitting in cars, or hanging around school or different places. Like that one guy who was at the funeral home — remember? He must have been assigned to us full-time for a while. I saw him just about everywhere."

Duncan felt he had to talk, act interested.

"Oh, yeah," he said. "One of those two guys that looked almost the same. Real sharp, with raincoats, wasn't it? Maybe you saw one of them half the time and the other the other half. They really looked a lot alike."

"No, not them," said Terry. "This was another one. Looked more like a barber, or a big jockey. Middle-aged. Sort of Spanish-looking. Maybe you didn't even see him."

And there it was. No big sirens going off, or light bulbs just above his head, but one moment Duncan had been putting together a bunch of let's-get-off-the-subject questions in his mind (How *is* Ben, anyway? When's school get over for the year? You got a summer job yet?) and the next moment he was actually sitting down on that little low oak table, staring at the tan rug that ran down the center of the hall, and feeling the black plastic of the telephone go greasy in his hand.

(What should he say? How about: "Oh, yes, I did. And, hey, guess what? The reason you haven't seen him for a while is that he's here in Burlington, most likely in the guest room, one flight down. Now isn't that amazing?" he could say.)

"Do you know the one I'm talking about?" Terry was asking the silence on the line.

"Maybe," Duncan said. "I'm not so sure. A lot of that's a blur — you know?" He sucked in one deep breath, real deep, and let it out again.

Terry must have thought he'd sighed.

"I know," she said. Her voice was round and soft. "And I'm sorry I even talked about it. I just wanted you to know that certain things are getting better, that's all. I've had a lot of time to think, the last few weeks, and I guess I know that it's never going to be the same as it used to, Duncan. And I guess that makes me sad, in certain ways. But what I also realize is that even when everything gets completely messed up . . . well, even then, I — a person — still has the same choice as before: to either try or not. No matter what, that doesn't change. It's my choice, my life, and I decide. . . ."

Duncan listened, heard the words that she was saying. His mind was pawing through a lot of different stuff — ideas and thoughts, reactions — as if his head was one big dresser drawer, and there was no light in the room.

Part of what he found was this: The little man downstairs had been there at Delaney's, had looked at him across the room; *that's* where he'd seen the guy before. That little man, now living in this house, now living in the Fetish guest room, was connected to his mother's and his brother's deaths, at least *some* way or

other. This little man who was — must be — a friend
of theirs, the Fetishes. A little man who'd stayed on
in New Jersey, checking out his house and Dottie's
house and Terry's house, his school. And now was
here in Burlington, and staying with the Fetishes.

Another part was what she'd just been saying: that
things were not the same. Between them, had she
meant? Or just in general? He felt relieved. But also
— weirdly — sad. And tender. Terry was a real good
kid, a gamer, hanging in there down the stretch,
whatever. She didn't fold or want a substitute, she
really didn't. And now she was saying:

". . . any plans yet? I mean, in time *or* place? I'm
sure you're okay and everything, but I just want to *see*
you." She laughed. "Same old nag, see, Duncan? I
could even come up there for a day or something, if
that'd be all right. Just so I *know*."

She didn't say what. That he was still in one piece?
That it was all over with them? Duncan didn't have
the slightest idea which one she meant. Or maybe
something different altogether.

"Well, I don't think you ought to do that right
now," he found himself saying. "This wouldn't be
that good a time. And anyway, I may be almost . . .
done with what I'm doing here. It could be just
another day or two, I'm not exactly sure. But maybe
if you call next week — provided I'm not back
already, which I might be. You want to do that, Tare?
I'd call *you*, except for the cops, but if they're looking
for me, still. . . . And next week, chances are. . . ."

"Okay, I'll do that, Duncan," Terry said. He

thought she sounded — strangely — satisfied. "I'll call you just about this time. And Duncan. . . ."

"Yes?" he said, just filling up the pause.

"You're still all right," she said. "I love you."

And she hung up before he could reply.

42. CONFUSIONS

Duncan went back to his room. Sky, from the bed, looked up; Duncan was staring at the floor. He went back to undressing, and when he was naked, he reached for his towel. But before he touched it, he shook his head and went over to the closet, got out running shoes and socks, and sweats. Sky wagged his tail: oh, yay, another outing.

When Duncan was all dressed again, they went downstairs and out the front door. There was Caitlin on the red stone steps, just coming in.

"Hi," she said. She smiled and cocked her head at him; her green eyes seemed to slant a little more than usual. "Going for a run — she brilliantly observed.

I'm glad. That means your back's all better, right? For which I claim full credit, as your therapist." She giggled.

Duncan found a smile, maybe fifteen watts' worth. "Uh-huh," he said. "I reckon that you should. It feels much better. As for the run" — he pointed down at Sky — "*he* talked me into it."

She started past him. "Well, enjoy," she said. "Perhaps I'll see you later. Dad's got to go to Clinton, and there was some talk about my going with him, but maybe I won't have to. I'm not sure." Clinton was where one of the larger NU-HU farms was, off in New York state.

Duncan touched her on the elbow, stopping her — then quickly took his hand away.

"Uh — who's that in your guest room, anyway?" he asked. "We almost ran him over on the stairs the other day, before I even realized he was staying with you. I didn't think I'd seen him around before." He thought that sounded okay. A little stupid, maybe, but all right. Casual, you *could* say; sure.

"Oh," she said. "He's worked for Dad for years; his name is Mister Carlo. Don't ask me where they ever met, originally. Or what he's doing in our guest room, as far as that goes; he's got his own apartment in Winooski. I guess it's maybe because he's been on the road a real long time and wants to be around familiar faces for a while. He travels a lot. My father says he's got a million contacts, not to mention super business sense. He calls him his 'short right arm.' He would, wouldn't he?" Of course she didn't mention which particular branch of the business the majority of Mister Carlo's contacts happened to be in. She bent and patted Sky.

"He's a sweet little guy, actually," she said. "And as loyal as they make 'em — kind of like our friend, here. There isn't anything he wouldn't do for my father, I don't think."

When she straightened up, Duncan was just turning away, pivoting on his left foot and picking up the other knee, way high, and pressing it against his chest. It was a stretch, a thing that's good to do before you run; he did it with the other leg, as well.

But before his head turned all the way, she saw his face for just a second — less than that. My God, she thought, this sweet young kid has got a "game face," just like Larry Bird, or someone. That same strange look, of almost frightening intensity. She hadn't noticed it when they'd been playing one-on-one. Maybe that had been like hacking around, for him. But now, this run was *training* — serious. Forget the smiles and sweetness; see you later.

She decided to go upstairs and ask her father what Mister Carlo *was* doing in the guest room, and how long he planned to stay. It was sort of a pain in the ass to have someone right *there*, a few doors down, if she was . . . entertaining.

Duncan didn't even think which way he'd rather go, when he first started — and so he stayed on Willard Street, just heading north, motoring along a good two miles before he realized where he was, and that he much preferred to run on dirt or grass, instead of city pavement. So, with that thought he changed direction, zigging east and zagging south; the University cross-country course was nice to run on, hard but very nice, and hard was fine with him, right then.

Sky just went along. He'd grown up on the streets, and so was traffic-wise, and didn't go charging across intersections without looking and waiting; he didn't need a person for his own protection. But, from time to time, he liked to touch eyes with his friend, to let him know that he was there and part of what was happening. Duncan liked that, too, and did it even then, although he didn't know he did, any more than he knew he watched the traffic and the lights himself, so as not to get run over. His conscious mind was totally absorbed with different thoughts and possibilities, reactions; they rumbled back and forth and back and forth and didn't just fill up his head until it almost burst, but also seemed to spill down in his chest, sometimes, and sit there, wet and woeful.

There was a chance (he thought) a very, very, good, good chance that this small man, this Mister Carlo person, had been what you might call *involved* in Brian's and his mother's deaths. Check that — why not face it? That Mister Carlo'd *killed* them (there, he'd said it) with a car bomb. The guy had been there at the wake, and then had hung around. And why? There *was* that thing you always heard about murderers going back to the scenes of their crimes. For some weird reason they actually seemed to do that. Had that been it? Could be. Of course, there was also that bullshit theory of Grunfeld's about how the people who killed Brian had probably planned to kill *him* at the same time. And would be looking for him later.

But that was just to scare him, saying that. I mean, come *on* (thought Duncan).

The only reason anyone'd have to kill Brian was something to do with drugs. That was obvious and uncontestable. All you had to do was read the papers and you'd know that people who dealt drugs got killed a lot. The Mafia — let's say — would not encourage competition. So Brian gets targeted because *somebody* (and it didn't have to be the Mafia) believes he's doing something that he oughtn't to. Breaking a rule — wasn't that ridiculous? Especially when his brother had been so determined — he'd told him that, a lot — to never make a wave, to always play it safe, back down, give no one reason to be mad at him.

"Hey," his brother'd said to him, "that there's the jungle, out there. You think I'm crazy, man? I don't *tease* the lions; thorn-removal is my business, buddy."

Sure, but sometimes in this world it isn't what you do that counts; it can be what some other person *thinks* you've done. Or even what that someone thinks you maybe plan on doing.

So, if Mister Carlo killed his brother (and his mother) for some drug-related reason, wouldn't that then mean that he — this Mister Carlo — was a drug-related person? Like working for a company ("the mob" seemed too ridiculous) competing with his brother? Like, NU-HU products, just for instance? Or a person competing with his brother, at the very least. Like Abraham Fetish, maybe?

Abraham Fetish. On the surface, just a plain, nice

guy. Friendly. Funny. Helpful. The guy had definitely gone out of his way to give Duncan some special help with his aura. And supposedly the lessons were working; he was doing it. According to Fetish, Duncan's everyday aura was noticeably different already, and when he concentrated, spectacularly different: blue-green, cool as glass. It hadn't taken them long, either, only a few sessions (with more planned where he could work on elasticizing the darn thing), but that had been time enough to convince Duncan that Fetish wasn't just doing it out of a sense of duty or anything, but that he actually liked him. And liked Sky, too. He knew a lot of different, far-out stuff, like the whole aura theory, but he was also very human, down to earth.

"I'm satisfied that this *does* work," he'd said to Duncan, once, "that people's auras are — *can* be — protective. At least for certain levels, at a certain range. But possibly the best part of our aura work is that it gives us *something* — every one of us that tries it. We put ourselves a little bit in charge again. Like the tribunes back in very early Rome we can — though poor and insignificant — shout, '*Veto*!': I forbid it. Gives all of us the sense that even at the worst of times, when nothing seems to work, *we* work — *we* matter."

So Duncan'd said to him, "But doesn't Nukismetic Humanism say that everything's completely fated, this whole big nuclear 'event,' this *war*, and lots of people fighting, dying, so's to make a better world? I mean, how can anyone defy fate?"

And Fetish only smiled at that, and maybe

winked, and said, "'Man who clenches fists not always best, when game is up for grabs.' Confusions 23:4."

Abraham Fetish. The way it looked to Duncan, right then, this man, this easygoing joker, was the one who'd ordered the bomb put in his brother's car by this other little man. ("There isn't *anything* he wouldn't do for my father, I don't think.") And that Fetish's reasons for giving that order were, simply, business reasons — no offense and nothing personal. *Of course* it wasn't the sort of thing he'd want to do. Oh, no. It just was done to, *a.* clean up a business situation, and *b.* send out a message to, like, *everyone* that this was what another business got, that messed or interfered with his.

What all this *also* meant, of course, was that he had, indeed, seen dope inside the NU-HU warehouse, as he'd thought he had. And that, beyond a shadow of a doubt, Caitlin Fetish was the biggest fucking liar-hypocrite in all this hopeless-little-*nothing*-of-a-fucked-up-rotten world.

43. QUESTION

Caitlin Fetish had stood on the stoop of the NU-HU house for about a count of ten, and watched as Sky and Duncan loped away, up Willard Street, one of them with dark green sweat pants on. Her upper teeth, with nothing else to do, had grabbed her lower lip, a corner of it, anyway. She'd seen a lot of other people wearing clothes that looked like Duncan's, but never anyone with that expression on his face. Not anyone with nothing on his mind but running, that's for sure. It wasn't any "game face," either — face it. The expression that she'd seen — why kid herself? — was more along the lines of . . . fury, shock, or hatred. Even all of the above. Not exactly the emotions you'd expect, or want, to see on the face of a lover of yours. Make that a teenaged lover of yours who was also about the sweetest person you'd ever met in your entire life.

In any case, she shrugged (a moment later) and bounded up the stairs. And when she reached the second floor, she headed for her father's room. One thing at a time. For now, the question was: What *was* Mister Carlo doing there?

Abraham Fetish was just zipping up his flight bag. The man was mortally afraid of airplanes and never, never traveled on the things, but he'd done a lot of fleeing with that bag.

"Why is Carlo here?" he said, repeating what his daughter had just asked, and trying to sound (by doing so) a little absentminded and professorish.

Stalling, Caitlin thought.

"Why is Carlo here?" her father asked again and picked his bag up off the bed. He shook his head. "No reason, really. I thought he might not — probably *would* not — have had the time. . . . That is to say, he wouldn't have had any *food* in his apartment. Refrigerator off, and all. It seemed it might be easier for him. . . . And, also — yes! — I think he said he wanted to get his rugs shampooed! It's like a service, where you call these people in, you know, and they spread that foam around, that makes the damnedest stink, for days. Place looks like a shaving cream commercial." He started for the door, his bag in hand.

"Look, sweatheart, gotta run," he said. "I should be back on Sunday. Mmmm-muh!" He bent and kissed her on the cheek.

"What's the hurry, Murray?" Caitlin said. "You're

just going to go to bed when you get there. You're not going to be able to *see* anything until morning. And besides, you seem so . . . *antsy*. Is our paint job wearing off, already?"

"No, no, no, no, no. No such thing," said Abraham. "Just got a ton of silly little details on my mind. 'De tail dogs de wag.' Dat's from Canines 17, verse 8, I do believe. So here I go; I'm off. *Adieu, adios, amo-amas-amat*. And all that rot."

Chuckling, he swept out the door and down the stairs.

44. ORA PRO NOBIS

Instead of going right down Willard Street and heading south on Shelburne Road, Abraham Fetish went the other way, the better to avoid the early evening traffic. That brought him past the Patrick Gym, the Field House, starting steeply down on Spear Street.

As usual, the shoulders of that street were dotted here and there with runners — men and women both, short and tall, young and old, even fat and skinny. A lot of people ran cross-country through the golf course to the end of it, and then attacked these steep, steep hills on Spear Street. "Gut-checks," he had heard them called.

Way ahead, he saw a runner with a dog, both coming up toward him — the runner tall and steady, laboring, the dog a lot less purposeful, sniffing here and there, then loping for a bit and catching up so easily. The pair were still a ways away when Fetish realized he knew them: Sky and Duncan, surely.

"Ah," he murmured, smiling, pleased to see them. He flicked the headlights of his big Mercedes on and off, three times. Duncan's head came up; he'd seen the signal, recognized the car.

Fetish raised his hand, saluting them, and got a shock that, although very different, was at least as big as last fall's earthquake, which was 5.2. Duncan's aura — even as the young man's eyes met his — was nothing like he'd ever seen before: a deep, deep, liquid, vicious red.

"Aura *pro nobis*," the large man muttered to himself, and grimaced at the pun.

What he'd said, as you may know, means (sort of): Pray for us.

45. WEIRD

Almost everyone that any one of us has ever known has had a parent (one or more) who seemed, to her or him, a little weird. And most of them, of us, adjust somehow (growing older helps) and love that parent anyway, regardless or (at times) because of that same weirdness.

Caitlin Fetish would have said amen to all of that. When it came to weirdness, her father had operated at a pretty high level for as long as she could remember, but she'd mostly liked the forms it took, and that, day in, day out, it made him so much different than the parents of her friends. In fact, Abraham Fetish was so weird that it sometimes seemed a little weird when he acted normal.

But it was hard for Caitlin Fetish to tell whether her father's evasiveness on the Mister Carlo question was normal, or not. All her life, different friends of hers complained to her about *their* parents' secretive, mendacious (even) attitudes, so possibly that *was* the norm (child, of parent, speaking). But it wasn't Abraham Fetish. He'd always given straight and honest answers to her questions, even toughies.

Years before, for instance, she and two best friends (and all sixth graders at the time) agreed to ask their fathers how old they were when they first "committed sexual intercourse" (their phrasing of the question cracked them up, repeatedly). Father A had answered it was absolutely none of daughter's business, and anyway completely off the subject which, as he recalled, was failing grades in French and tardiness to meals. Father B said, "A good deal older than you are right now, young lady. A very, very great deal older. Ask me every year or so; I'll let you know when you get close, if you're still interested." But Abraham Fetish answered, "Let's see. Twenty years, ten months, three days, I think it was. Somewhere in that neighborhood." And Caitlin'd said, "Why'd you wait so long?" And he'd said, "I'm not sure." She'd nodded, understanding that, and he'd said, "What are *your* plans?" And she'd said she certainly didn't have any at the moment, and he'd said, "Good. It's best to be a little . . . *wary*." She'd remembered that a long, long time, had been (oh, very) wary, and was glad.

So she was definitely ill-at-ease when Abraham'd just grabbed his bag and headed out the door before he'd told her what the story was with Carlo. What the whole, true story was, that is. Could his attitude, she wondered, connect in any way with Duncan's curiosity? With Duncan's unfamiliar face when *he* sped down the street? She was still . . . *uncomfortable* about the fact that Brian, Duncan's brother (who was killed) had had her father's name in his belongings — had wanted him to be "checked out" by Duncan. Why on earth would that be? Conceivably, her father could have owed him money; maybe that was it. He couldn't have wanted Duncan to work for her father, could he? That didn't seem to make a lot of sense. Duncan had a healthy-looking future on his own: college, playing ball, the ordinary things he seemed to like and be so good at. Why give that up at seventeen or so? How big a nut had brother Brian been?

What she absolutely refused to consider for even a moment, because it was so completely impossible and absurd, was that Brian might have thought that her father was planning to kill him. Weird? Oh, sure, why not? But not a murderer. Not in a radioactive lifetime, Caitlin Fetish thought. But her thinking that, her *knowing* that, had nothing much to do with anything that Duncan might be thinking. He surely had had something on his mind that wasn't very pleasant.

She felt a little weird herself, a little batty. I need a change of scene, she thought, some different dialogue — perhaps a different set of characters.

She went to her study, dialed the phone, and had Lisle paged, up at the hospital. He was an acting intern for that month, in surgery, which put him (as he'd never say) in something called hog heaven.

"Lisle Hardaway," is what he did say, when he came on the phone. He'd learned to say his name so that it sounded crisp, efficient, confident, yet friendly. The perfect doctor's voice, he thought.

"Oh, Doctor Hardaway," she said. "I've got this case of malnutrition, here. Medical attention is required, I'm afraid — at once. I think I can get the patient down to Zachary's, if you can order them to get an IV ready, pepperoni-anchovy, I think, with — "

"Caitlin," he cut in. "I'm sorry but I can't. We've had a flood of new admissions in the last half hour, and I'm afraid I'm up to my . . . my. . . ."

"*Elbows*, I feel sure," she said. "You surgeons. Well, okay. Just remember that I asked. That counts as one for me, so now it's your turn. Don't make me wait for summer rates or anything, all right?"

As has been said, Lisle Hardaway was not a stupid man. Plus, he'd been trained to ask the probing, pointed question. "Are you okay?" he said. "You sound a little — "

"Funny," she provided. "But, yeah. I'm perfectly all right. Imperfectly all right, as Carlo'd say. You know how it gets down here, from time to time. But nothing serious. I'll see you sometime soon. Whenever. Enjoy. Set a leg." And she hung up.

Hardaway put down the phone and stood there for a moment, looking at his clean right hand, still holding the receiver. It had done a perfect job of hanging up, precise and elegant, he thought. When he got off duty, if it wasn't too absurdly late, he'd take a spin by Caitlin's house. She'd sounded just a little odd, for sure.

Caitlin thought she'd go for pizza anyway, but first (she also thought) she'd leave a note in Duncan's room. She went upstairs, and down the hall, and knocked.

"Come in," said Christopher.

She did, and found him standing, all dressed up, before the mirror. He had a dark blue blazer on, pinched in at the waist, a yellow shirt and shiny silver tie with thin black stripes in it. His pants were gray-flared double knits, his shoes were rubber-soled black saddles.

Caitlin Fetish whistled, bugged her eyes, raised both hands, and staggered back a step.

"Oh, cut it out," said Christopher. She noticed that his hair shone, too. "It's just my parents are in town. Or not in town, in Middlebury, as a matter of fact. So I said I'd take the bus down and have dinner with them at the Dog Team. Which of course meant that my mother insisted I spend the night with them, at the inn. Give her an inch and she tries to talk a kilometer, I swear. One of these times I expect her to come with a deprogrammer and lock me in a room at the Radisson, till I repent."

"Well, you look *very* nice," Caitlin said, and Christopher blushed and snuck another ogle at the mirror. "I'm just going to leave your roomie a note, and then

I'll get out of your way. Got a scrap of something I can write on?"

Christopher obliged, then saying he was late, he hurried out the door. Everyone's in such a rush, but me, thought Caitlin.

She wrote: "D. Come down and see me sometime, like after you've taken your tub; drying-off is optional. You just won a million dollars in a special random drawing in the Vermont state lottery, and I want to be the one to tell you. Adoringly, C. P.S. April Fool. But I do have a bag of those little Milky Ways."

She stuck the note in one of Duncan's boots, and put the boot on his pillow. That note was much more normal and relaxed than she was feeling. She definitely felt weird.

46. REVOLTING REVELATION

Mister Carlo had tried to convince himself that he hadn't seen the brother of "the man who'd gotten in the accident" (as he liked to think of Brian; he refused to think of Ruth at all). Sometimes, he believed he'd done it, too — that he'd succeeded, that he *knew* that kid was nowhere in Vermont. How could he be?

But even then he'd think: Well, why not go and take a nice look out the window? Couldn't do no harm. There's no one out there that he wouldn't want to see — right? Right. And just to prove it, he would go and stand beside his window for a while, like half an hour, looking down the path, the driveway leading up to NU-HU house. He kept the curtain's edge between his fingers, by his face, because . . . because he liked the silky feel of the material.

When Caitlin Fetish, seeing him through his open door as she passed down the hall, walked noiselessly into his room, put her hands over his eyes, and said in an affected voice, "Guess who?" he simultaneously (a) let out a scream that could have scared the shell off a Galapagos tortoise, (b) leaped almost out of his pointy patent-leathers, and (c) started to flail the air with his fists as if he were playing the maracas at a fast-rhumba contest judged by Salvadoran sergeants at the edge of a ravine.

Caitlin, unprepared for *that* reaction, took some quick steps backward, saying, "Carlo. Easy, boy," and keeping both hands up and open, to fend him off, if need be.

Of course she didn't have to. Once he turned around and got his eyes to focus and his mouth to move, he stopped the punching, shook his head, and babbled, "Caitlin! Christmas, what you do that for? I'm thinking that you're *him*, for peace sake!" At which point he sank down on the edge of his bed, covered up his face, and sobbed hysterically.

About ten minutes later, Caitlin Fetish could have done the same. The story of what happened in New Jersey had come pouring out of Carlo, all of it: the order he'd misunderstood, Ruth's and Brian's awful deaths, his panic and confusion, his failed attempts to find "the brother," and his flight back up to Burlington. And now his fear that the brother had discovered who he was, and where — and had come up to Vermont to kill him.

If Caitlin's mind had been able to work normally,

she might have said and done a lot of things she
didn't, I should think. She might, for instance, have
insisted Carlo move to a motel — have *taken* him to
one — and then made sure that she saw Duncan, told
him what she knew, and asked him what *he* knew, the
moment he came in the house. In another state of
mind, she might have functioned as the keeper of the
peace, the arbitrator — the powerful, respected, neutral force that bandages the awful wounds and shows
all sides that nothing's to be gained by thoughts of
vengeance, hatred, and the like.

But for the moment she was simply stunned. The
horror overwhelmed her. It wasn't that her moral
compass failed her (as, sadly, it's been known to do,
when people feel big pressure); what happened was:
Her motor flooded, stalled. Poor people who'd been
killed! (she thought). Poor Duncan! Poor Mister
Carlo and her father, too! The total dreadfulness. . .
nobody meant . . . *et cetera.* Poor her — what could
she, should she, do? No wonder her father had
agreed, so readily, to get out of the drug business! No
wonder he was running around like a chicken without a head! No wonder Mister Carlo was absolutely
freaked!

And no wonder — she thought this later on —
Duncan looked as if he'd like to kill somebody.

She never did tell Mister Carlo that yes, indeed,
the brother of the man he'd killed was living in a room
just one flight up.

47. HIGH WITNESS

She almost might as well have. Within the hour, Mister Carlo, standing at his window, watched while Sky and Duncan walked up to the house, both panting just a little.

There wasn't any doubt whatever, this time — absolutely none. *He* was the one who'd seen the boy at the funeral home, not Abe; *he* was the high witness. And now, standing on the second floor and looking down (as they came up the path) he was again.

When Sky and Duncan reached the second floor, and kept on going to the third, Mister Carlo watched them through his door — himself on hands and knees, the door now open just a crack. As soon as they had passed, he left his room and slipped downstairs and oh-so-casually confessed to Justin (Bertram? Roger?) he'd forgotten where "that lovely puppy dog" was living. Third floor, and take a left? The last room on the left? Of *course*.

He thanked the man, continued to the kitchen. From three inside a drawer, he chose a rolling pin, a nice big heavy one. Next, he tried to find some burger or a bone, but couldn't. He settled for a jar of peanut butter. Then he went back to his room.

Peanut butter might not buy an ally (is the way he figured it), but should be good enough for nonalignment.

48. FLYING BLIND

Terry Bissonette had boarded the People Express flight for Burlington, out of Newark, New Jersey, still wondering just who the hell she thought she was. It was usually her mother who raised that particualr question, traditionally with "young lady" on the end of it, and (of course) not wanting any answer, make that "back-talk." But now she put it to herself.

Was this unaccustomed activist just good old Trusty Terry, faithful friend, a hundred and eleven pounds of loyalty, and love . . . and *intuition*, folks? A girl who wasn't scared to put her body on the line, who didn't goop around and whine, "Oh, what's the use?"

Or was she Terry Troublesome (a teenaged turkey), the hypocrite and show-off (yes!) who made a big display of caring and commitment, while really (merely) stroking ego, to the point of you-know-what? Which everybody does sometimes, let's face it, even good girls (Terry Tiresome informed herself).

She really didn't know. It all went back to the phone call, of course.

When Terry hung up the phone at the end of her talk with Duncan, she swept her remaining quarters off the little metal shelf and into her bag and walked away from the booth feeling great. But after she'd gone a block or so, she realized that what was making her feel good was having made the call at all — that and hearing Duncan's voice, knowing he was there (somewhere that had a number she could dial), and that she'd reached him. Along about then, some of what he'd said came back to her, and she started to get this funny feeling, kind of itchy and excited, very different than the sort of *down* that she'd been trapped in.

She changed direction, went to Dottie's house; it was the only logical place to go. She'd spent a lot of time there right after Duncan left, but not so much the last two weeks or so. It wasn't that Dottie had gotten any less friendly, just more solemn, you might say, and quieter. But now she needed Dottie as a sounding board.

"I'm pretty sure he said, 'This wouldn't be a real good time,'" she said. They'd settled in the kitchen. "And then, 'I may be just about through with what I came up here for.' What do *you* think he meant by that?"

Dottie stirred the coffee in her mug, a big white mug with a red number "1" on the side of it.

"Lord, I don't know," she said. "But just as a wild guess, it could be he's involved in . . . I don't know, some sort of *project*, maybe, don't you think? Something that has a beginning and a middle and an end, from the sound of it. Maybe he's building some shelves at the health food store." She thought that sounded pretty sappy, but she said it anyway; anything was possible, for God's sake. "What do *you* think it is?" She didn't look at Terry.

"Well," Terry said, "when he went up there, he told both of us the same thing: that he was going because Brian wanted him to — and so that maybe he could get his head together and feel better, right?"

Dottie nodded. They'd said that back and forth to each other quite a number of times after Duncan left, as if the more they said it the more it'd seem like a great idea. And, from Dottie's point of view, the more insistently they said it, the less likely Terry might be to grope around for other reasons/explanations. As she now, apparently, had done.

"But just suppose," Terry was saying, excitedly, "he really had something completely different in mind, that he didn't want to tell us, because he thought we might worry, or something. Suppose he really knew who this Fetish was, all along. Suppose Fetish was a business associate of Brian's. Then, couldn't it be that Duncan was going up there to try and — I don't know how to say this — and get Brian's share of the business? I don't mean *merchandise* or anything, but maybe get paid some money that Brian was owed and that'd rightfully belong to him? Wouldn't that make sense?"

"Well, I don't know," Dottie said. She was absolutely convinced, in her own mind, that Duncan hadn't known who Fetish was before he'd gone to Burlington — she knew from the way he'd talked about the note — but she didn't see any harm in letting Terry think that he did. It'd give a harmless explanation of what he'd said to her on the phone. He obviously hadn't mentioned the girl, and she sure as hell wasn't going to either. Whatever was going to happen was going to happen. Duncan was a great kid, but with men you never knew, thought Dottie. Harry Michalis had been a great kid, too.

"It'd make sense for him to want what was rightfully Brian's," Dottie went on. "I don't think he found more than a little *change* in Brian's room. And as far as 'merchandise' goes" — she made a little shrug and smiled a little smile — "we know there wasn't any here. They sure did search for some. Everybody took a shot at *that*."

But Terry wasn't out of theories yet.

"Of course the other possibility that hit me," she then said, "was that maybe Duncan's found out something about — *you* know — who did it. That maybe this Fetish person knew something about who was responsible, let's say. And if Duncan got ahold of information like that, I'm not at all sure he wouldn't try to . . . do something. You know how he can get, like really stubborn and intense? Well, that's the way he sounded. And you know how responsible he is — right? — his sense of duty? I know he isn't violent, or that type of thing — a violent *person*, you know — but if he got this information, and he thought they'd maybe get away, unless . . . I'm just afraid that with his emotions all involved like that, and nobody with him, no real friend or anyone to help him. . . ." Terry picked at the side of her thumb with her forefinger nail. She was more than halfway hoping that Dottie would say something along the lines of what she was thinking herself, about what the right thing was for a person in this situation to do, and about women not just staying on the sidelines all the time and leading cheers, and junk like that.

Instead, however, Dottie shook her head.

"Uh-uh," she said. "I don't believe that for a minute. Not what you said about Duncan, but the part about those people up there having anything to do with Ruth and Brian. Listen, I'll tell you the truth — that's what I was worried most about, when he left. I didn't see any sense in bringing it up to you at the time — and he was determined to go — so I didn't. But those people are *kooks*, that's what they are! I was so relieved when he told me they were into health food stores and auras and called themselves the Nukismetic Humanists, I almost jumped up and down in that phone booth, I swear. You know, I've hung out with folks like that for almost all my life. Take it from me — they're harmless, at least to anybody else. I mean, think whatever you want, but face it — there's a hundred other things that Duncan could have meant." But she didn't suggest any more of them, especially any having to do with the girl who was so "crazy about Sky," and six feet tall, and "you should see her."

"The good thing" — Dottie babbled on — "is that a week from now you'll know. From what you said he said, the waiting's almost over, even sooner than we figured." Dottie finally smiled and shrugged and raised both palms. Cross your fingers and your toes, my girl, she thought.

So Terry smiled right back and then stood up and hurried home; there, she made some calls and left her mom a note. She often spent the night at Jennifer's.

Flying through the night when you didn't know exactly who the hell you (thought you) were was definitely a little scary, Terry thought. Especially when you were going to a place you'd never been before to try to deal with something that very well might turn out to be a figment of your own imagination. But. . . .

Dottie might know kooks from A to Z, but *she* knew Duncan better. Didn't she? Better than anyone?

49. MISTAKES

Abraham Fetish drove south on Route 22-A, all the way to Fair Haven, Vermont, where he picked up Route 4, west; that took him into New York state. He dined, a little late but heartily, in Saratoga Springs, and when he'd finished with his meal, he got back in his car, and turned around, and headed back the way he'd come.

Somewhere in the chocolate cheescake, everything had come together in a lump below his breastbone: thick corn chowder, batter-dipped fried chicken (yams and beans) with double salad (dressing by the house), and (heavier than all of those) the feeling Mister Carlo had been right. The brother of the guy they'd accidentally killed *had* come to Burlington, *was* in his house, and furious and vengeful. Six foot three, and answering to "Duncan."

Those deaths had been an accident; God knew; this boy was the survivor of the accident. Maybe it'd have been better if they'd all been in that car, the three of them, the whole damn family. That wouldn't have made it any sadder, or any bigger a mistake (thought Fetish, groaning inwardly — was this his mind with thoughts like those inside of it?). If you're going to make a mistake of that magnitude, in that particular area (thought Abraham Fetish, known to his friends as a humorous and sentimental, kindly man), it could conceivably be a lot . . . *safer*, if it's a whopper.

Now, if anything happened to Caitlin. . . .

50. PIZZA

Caitlin Fetish did go out for pizza. The way she figured it, she had to eat — she'd *better* eat — so maybe she should carbo-load a little. It wasn't only energy she needed, but endurance, too; she saw no easy times ahead. Did pizza qualify as carbohydrate? Well, she guessed it did; spaghetti did, so pizza ought to. And she always thought of pizza as a treat, a pizza down at Zachary's. She could use a treat; she really felt messed up.

She sat by herself in a two-person booth and listened to the sounds around her: bursts of laughter, muddled conversations, steelware on formica, clink of Molson's bottle neck on glass. She asked the waitress for a small sausage pizza and a Pepsi Cola.

In the booth behind her, a girl was saying to another girl: "The only thing to do is just sit down and tell him, very calmly, what you think. . . ."

Caitlin heard that and looked at her hands. They were clenched together in the center of her place mat. She opened them and laid them flat and looked at them some more. There probably wasn't any sitting down and telling Duncan, very calmly, what she thought. As soon as he found out the truth about . . . (she bobbed her head) *what happened* — which he may have done already, somehow, going by his face — everything between them would be changed, disgusting. He'd have to see her as a part of "them," the ones that did it. And she could never look at him and not feel awful.

Okay, she'd always known their love affair would end, at some point, and there'd be some feeling-bad involved. But no regrets, is what she'd told herself. Up to now, she hadn't ever stopped to think of *hatred*.

The waitress said, "Excuse me," and she moved her hands and smiled the automatic smile of someone being fed. The pizza looked enormous; she couldn't eat all that. Lisle said that was what she always said, and *he'd* say, "Pizza's two-dimensional — there isn't all that much." She took a sip of her drink.

She hated the idea of being hated, by anyone. Of course she had her faults and annoying qualities, but she really did try to be honest and fair and considerate. None of that mattered; most people'd say the exact same things about themselves, probably. She was going to be hated, by someone she loved — and who certainly had loved her, no question about it.

That seemed like the most unfair and stupid thing imaginable.

She picked up a slice of the pizza and bit into the end of it without thinking and of course burned the roof of her mouth, just behind her top front teeth. More stupidity, she thought.

Usually, she thought, the hatred comes first, and then you get the killing. In this case, it was the other way around. Nobody'd hated Duncan's mother or his brother, but that bomb had killed them just as dead as if someone (or a lot of people) had. The whole thing started by accident, but still you get the hatred, anyway. Once somebody's killed, you're always going to get it, and what's more, you've maybe got a cycle going. No one wants to let those someones "get away with" anything.

Shit, she thought. Those fucking *idiots*.

She put the pizza slice back down. So what might Duncan do? She hadn't even thought of that, before. At the very least, he'd want to see someone in jail for, well, forever, probably. But at the very worst he'd want to do something himself. That would be more the way an athlete would look at it. He'd want to show them, want a rematch, want the ball, the final shot. The crowd, the coaches would expect it of him — some action to regain his self-respect. Coaches loved to preach that concept: self-respect.

She was glad her father had gone to Clinton. But there was still Mister Carlo, little creep (she thought). She took another bite of pizza. It had cooled down a lot, but the burn on the roof of her mouth still hurt. She'd gone from feeling weird to feeling sad and feeling pissed, she realized — probably a typical rotation. What a world, she thought. Why not just say fuck it, and forget it?

She put some money on the table, then piled the pizza slices on top of each other and folded them in a napkin. What a soggy mess, she thought. Why am I doing this? she asked herself.

She took the pizza with her, anyway.

51. "JUSTICE"

Duncan's run had done a lot for him, just the way they say a run is meant to do. ("They" are almost always boring runners, have you noticed?) Aside from improving his muscle tone and keeping the protective calluses on his feet up to standard, and getting rid of certain body wastes by means of heavy perspiration, that run might very well have added to his life span. In two ways, as a matter of fact. Way one was the benign effect on his cardiovascular system, which, in anyone, can always stand some good aerobic exercise. Way two was that perhaps the run, by burning up adrenalin and giving him some time to think, and tiring him out a little, may have stopped him from charging right into Mister Carlo's room and possibly getting stabbed to death by that small *hombre* in the mother of a panic.

Instead, he'd gone up to his room and taken, as he'd planned to do some time before, a good, hot shower. Of course he'd seen his boot, with Caitlin's note in it, the second he'd come in the room. Partly, that was due to Christopher's and his contrasting beds. You see, the first thing in the morning, soon as he got up, Duncan made his bed. And once that bed was made, he never used it as a place to put his clothes or books — or boots, whatever. Sky never had to worry when he jumped on it; the bed was always smooth and clear as the deck of an aircraft carrier. Christopher, however — so neat and organized in every other way — never made his bed, his waterbed, at all. Even on the day he changed his sheets it was a mess, mounded high with anything he owned, from vests to volleyballs. So the thing was: If you put anything at all on Duncan's bed — never mind a boot, a *bobbie pin* — he'd notice it at once, while Chris's could absorb a . . .kangaroo.

Duncan wasn't sure just what to make of Caitlin's note. His best guess was: She just was being cool, assuming he'd been taken in by . . . everything. He couldn't believe what a liar she'd turned out to be, and how big a sucker she must think he was. But even considering that, he wasn't sure he wanted to confront her. Not quite yet, anyway. What seemed to make more sense — *strategic* sense — to him was to go down to her father's study and do another job on it. But not the walls, this time. Somewhere in the Fetish desk, or files, there must be something — evidence —

to hook him up with drugs and Brian; Duncan was convinced of that. Fetish was away, so he could go down there and take his time and make a thorough search for what he needed. He'd leave a note for Chris and tell him he was at the movies, the Woody Allen double feature at the Nick; that would make it clear — convincing, too — why Sky was in the room. When he found the evidence, he'd simply turn it over to the cops. Let the whole damn bunch of them just rot in jail forever; he'd be done with them, long gone.

On his run he'd thought about that side of it: the justice part, the vengeance part — whatever you wanted to call it. He'd discovered that in terms of what he, himself, was capable of doing, he didn't have a whole hell of a lot of choice. There wasn't any way in the world that he could take some weapon in his hands and use it on those people: on Caitlin or on Abraham — even on little Mister Carlo, who was probably the actual killer, and whom he'd never really even spoken to.

Duncan wondered what that made him. Civilized? Humane? Or chicken and contemptible? There were probably a lot of guys (most guys?) who, faced with their mother's or their brother's murderers, would throw a fit and grab a club, an ax, a knife, a gun and just . . . go at 'em. Would think that was their duty (and their pleasure, in a weird way, more or less). An eye for an eye, and all that jazz. Was there something wrong with him for not, like, *jumping* at the chance he had?

How about (he'd asked himself) if he could do it from a distance, like with a rifle, where he wouldn't even see the wounds he made, or the looks on their faces? Or from an even farther distance, like throwing the switch for an electric chair in another city, or dropping a bomb from a plane on a place he knew they were? That probably wouldn't bother most people a whole lot. Justice seemed to get a lot easier to dispense the farther away you get and the less you know the evil-doers — *animals* — you justiced. When the distance gets far enough, or the people different enough (religion, color, language, or whatever), or best of all, both, it almost gets to be a cinch to justice them. It serves the bastards right (is what you're meant to say).

So what was the matter with *him?* (Duncan asked himself again). He didn't seem to have whatever stuff it took to play avenging angel. But was there really such an angel? In whose heaven was that? Duncan asked himself. Well, he'd always thought that nothing really worked. Why the hell should he be Sir Exception?

He'd kept saying those things to himself and asking himself those questions so he didn't even have to think about Caitlin and all he'd never ever do with her, to her, because of her, again.

He wrote the note and put it on his bed beside the dog and ordered Sky to "stay." The guy just barely lifted up his head and then lay down again, one tired dog.

52. EVENING SKY

The thing about Sky was: He was a dog.

He was very interested in food and shelter and, from time to time, in sex, but there wasn't lots of other stuff he wanted, if you don't count love.

He very much enjoyed a run across a field, the leap to catch a Frisbee in his mouth, but never once compared his running, leaping, catching to another dog's.

He had no point of view, in this sense: no desire to convince a lot of other dogs to live a certain way, or force them to, if need be; anyone could be like him who wanted to; he didn't get into arguments about it.

If he or Duncan were attacked, he'd fight all right, but not to kill; he'd never start a fight, bite first.

He didn't know anything about bombs, and frankly, wasn't interested.

And he's the only major character in this book who was thoroughly enjoying himself, that early evening.

53. COUNTDOWN

Mister Carlo laid out all his weapons in a row on his bed. They were, with one exception perhaps, a pretty traditional, even conventional, group of killers.

First, there was a knife, a part of a carving set his sister had given him a number of years before; it had a bone handle and was made of stainless steel. He'd never been able to get it real, *real* sharp, but it had a good point on the end of it, and it was certainly a lot sharper than a ton of other things that he could think of. It was a lot sharper than an egg-beater, for instance.

Next to the knife, he put his rope. Ah-ha, he thought, real quality item, good as they come; we're talking *rope*, not clothesline, or like that: the brown coarse, *ropey* stuff, made out of juke — whatever. A friend had brought it over once, to Mister Carlo's place, to tie his dog outside, and when he'd left he had forgotten it, or something. Mister Carlo didn't one hundred percent believe that any dog was incapable of a "mistake," no matter how well trained it was, no matter what its record was over how many years of not doing it indoors. It could happen: canine error. This particular rope was a lot longer than he needed for strangling someone (unless the "someone" was an elephant, let's say), but Mister Carlo figured that was all right. He could use the part of the rope he needed, and the rest would just *be* there, to make sure, in case he needed it. You could always tie a dog with it, for instance.

Beside the knife and the rope he had his hammer, a standard Stanley, the kind that had a metal handle, rubber grip, and so forth. At other times he'd used that hammer for nonviolent purposes: to put up pictures, crush ice, bang on the radiator (a total waste of time in that the landlord lived in Colchester, not in the basement) and, occasionally, force pieces into a jigsaw puzzle. It certainly *could* be an effective weapon in a game of "It's either him or me," but he was a little concerned about the small size of the striking surface. It had no more than a medium-sized head, at the very best.

The rolling pin, however, next to it, his most recent discovery, seemed like an absolutely first-class knocker-outer. It had a lot of striking surface, about the most of any weapon you could think of, right up there with the baseball bat. Get in the first blow with a rolling pin and "it's all over butter shrouding," Mister Carlo thought. And — Mister Carlo's eyes widened delightedly — there, right next to the rolling pin, was a *pillow*! He could knock out the boy with the rolling pin, then cover-smother-up with that nice pillow. He wouldn't even have to look while you-know-what was happening. Compared to almost anything, the pillow was a nice, clean weapon.

A couple of minutes with the old pillow and (Mister Carlo told himself) it'd be "him" (that's "me," that's "*he*"), once and for all.

Duncan went quietly down the main staircase, staying way over to one side, his back and hands against the wall. When he reached the second floor, he glanced at the guest room door. He could see light underneath it, and he heard a faint sound from within the room. It was impossible to guess what made that particular noise, which really didn't sound like anything he'd heard before, in his entire life. But then, how many people (after all) have ever heard peanut butter being scooped into a soap dish with a bone-handled carving knife?

He kept on going, slid down the hall to Abraham Fetish's study. Once inside, he put the towel from around his neck along the bottom of the door; he'd fooled his mother with that trick for years — or so he thought, at least. Then he sat down at the desk and started opening the drawers.

The big Mercedes made good time, boring northward through the night: a heavy, handsome, dark green toad on wheels. It zoomed straight up the Northway to Glens Falls, then turned and found Route 4 again.

Its driver (Fetish, Abraham) was trying to think about anything other than the possibility that this tall boy (Duncan) with the angry aura might just decide that what was bad for his mother and brother would also be just terrible for a Fetish daughter. Surely people didn't think along those lines, not north of Appalachia, anyway (so Fetish tried to tell himself). But Ireland, there, was north of Appalachia (Fetish thought) and Banigan — which must be his last name — did not sound Swiss. . . .

Fetish struck his forehead one sharp blow, and got another station in his mind. Was there *any* chance that he (that's Caitlin's Dad) might *not* end up in jail, when this was finally over? Much as he might hate to call himself by such a small, unnecessary, even gaudy name, the word *accessory* (to murder) seemed to fit the case. And accessories, he knew, got put away. How could he defend himself in court? "But, gee, I didn't *mean* it . . . ," certainly seemed weak and lacking . . . something, Fetish thought.

"But not *conviction*, though," he said out loud. "I think that that defense would *guarantee* conviction." Fetish laughed a very hollow laugh and eased up on the gas a trifle. It would never do to have the prosecutor say, and prove, he was a man with no respect for laws, however trivial. "A *criminelle habituelle*, the sort for Devil's Island," he could hear the fellow saying, nastily.

Then he had another thought. The old insanity defense was not without its charms, its possibilities. He ran a finger around his neck, inside his collar, and tried to cross his eyes.

"Never mind psychiatrists, your honor," he whined. "Ask anyone who's ever known me." That didn't sound too bad, to him.

Then he thought about Caitlin again, and the danger she might possibly be in.

"Damn the torpedoes," he muttered. "And the ICBM's as well. Not to mention Smokey's little radar traps."

His broad and generally cheerful face looked worn and haggard, as the car leaped forward.

When Mister Carlo left his room, carrying the rolling pin, the rope, the bed pillow, and the soap dish full of peanut butter, he turned right rather than left and headed down the hall toward Caitlin's rooms. He knew, from other visits in the house, that he could open up a door at that end of the hall (next to her study door, in fact) and find, behind it, wooden stairs. That was the servants' staircase in the olden days, going up and down. And taking it (if he went up) would bring him out quite close to Duncan's door, as well as minimize the chance that he'd be seen by other Friends.

He started up, indeed was halfway to his destination before he found this question in his head: Wouldn't it be better — much, much better — to wait until he could be pretty sure that Duncan was asleep?

And, after it, this answer: Surely, yes, for peace

sake. Knocking out a person with a rolling pin who was asleep (already) was probably at least one hundred eighty-three percent easier than knocking out a person who was wide awake (and had his hands around your throat, for instance).

He nodded, stopped, and almost started down again. But then he thought: Why not, better, he should stay right where he was? No one ever, hardly ever, took that way of going up and down. And furthermore, if Duncan had, by any chance, decided it was either him or *him*, that night, and got into (broke in, attacked, or fire-bombed) his room . . . well, then, he wouldn't be there! He'd be safe and sound, just calmly sittin' on Astaire. Then, later on. . . .

Mister Carlo put his pillow down and sat on it. He was a good waiter. It was just too damn bad he'd ever left the restaurant business. If you got an order wrong at *La Paloma* you could lose a tip, but it wouldn't be the end of the world.

Caitlin Fetish went straight to her own part of the second floor, when she got back to the house. First of all, she thought that Duncan might be there, and also she didn't want to put down that soggy napkin full of pizza slices anywhere but on the edge of the sink in her bathroom. When she'd discovered that Duncan wasn't in any of her other rooms, she put down the pizza, washed her hands, and went back into her study to think for a moment.

It didn't take her long to decide that there were some things for her to *do* — that she *should* do — no matter how unpleasant they might very well turn out to be.

Talk to Duncan. Talk to Mister Carlo. Make sure that everyone both heard and understood the truth of what had happened (she hoped that she could add *believed* to *heard* and *understood*). Maybe get Mister Carlo out of the house. Certainly disarm anyone who'd armed himself in any way at all.

She headed for Duncan's room first.

The room was dark when she opened the door, but enough light came in from the hall for her to see the shape of Chris's bed in front of her (Duncan's was around behind the door). Amazingly (but typically) it *looked* as if Chris was asleep in his bed — the mound of mess, as usual. Of course she knew he wasn't, so she didn't hesitate to walk right in and find the lamp by Duncan's bed and turn it on. Sky looked up at her and thumped his tail, and yawned.

The boot with the note in it was gone, but there on the bed, right next to Sky, was Duncan's note to Christopher. She read it, pursed her lips; she looked down at her watch. It'd still be more than a couple of hours before he got back from the movies. Fine, in a way. She'd just get Mister Carlo moved into the Holiday Inn, and then she could check the movie times in the paper and wait up until Duncan got back.

She patted Sky, frowned at the tangle of clothes and other junk on Chris's bed (including vest *and* volleyball), and went on out the door.

Sky had been dreaming when Caitlin Fetish

opened the door, but of course he'd waked up at once and recognized her smell, and step, and style — and then relaxed again.

In his dream, he and another dog he didn't recognize (and who didn't even seem to speak his language) were both chasing after the same huge flock of winged jelly doughnuts. The doughnuts seemed to come in various shapes and sizes, and although they flapped their wings a lot, they couldn't seem to fly. They only rushed around, this way and that, with jelly oozing out of their fat little bodies.

Neither he nor the other dog was having a lot of luck with the chase, though, because any time that one of them got close to a doughnut, the other one would veer off course and snap at him, and the first dog would have to worry more about his own safety than his catch. It was sort of ridiculous (not to mention frustrating) how much time he had to spend defending himself, instead of eating jelly doughnuts, or making friends with them. So he hadn't been all that displeased at being waked up.

He hoped that he'd have better luck next dream.

Down in Mister Carlo's room, Caitlin found the same number of people she was looking for as she had in Duncan's room, namely zero. It was an empty room; nobody home, not even a dog on a bed.

But on the bed, in lieu of dog (and note) there was a grim array of weapons. From left to right: a hammer (Stanley, metal-handled) and a carving knife (bright stainless steel). But whoa, that stainless blade was streaked, as if it had been lately wiped, but hastily.

Caitlin wrinkled up her nose and sniffed — and then relaxed. She didn't think it had been used to *stab* somebody.

"Unless the person went to grade school and had just had lunch," she said out loud — and blushed to realize what she'd said. So she also said, "You're sick, you know that?" to herself. But the knife *did* smell of peanut butter, unmistakably. And yes, there on the dresser was an open jar of same. Mister Carlo must have made himself a snack before he went wherever he had gone. She wondered where the little man could be.

"I guess this calls for another note," she said, out loud again. "You'd think this was the White House. Or a fourth-grade classroom." And she sniggered.

She found a piece of Nukismetic Humanism stationery in the writing table drawer and wrote the following:

> Señor:
>   It necessitates I see you on a matter
>   of the greatest urgency imaginable.
> Come to my room the same moment that
>   you read this, *por favor. Pronto, pronto,*
>   *pronto.*
>   With a thousand good wishings,
>   Caitlin

She then stuck the bone handle of the carving knife into the peanut butter and impaled the note on its point. She placed the jar, with the knife and note sticking out of it, in the middle of the floor.

267

Then she went back to her room and settled down to wait. Judging by the movie times that were given in the paper, it looked as if Duncan wouldn't be Woody-Allened-out until well after eleven. There was no telling when Carlo might come back. She absolutely couldn't *imagine* where he might have gone, and why he'd eaten peanut butter before he went there. That didn't seem like a very Spanish thing to do.

It took Duncan a couple of hours to go through Abraham Fetish's desk, and the file cabinets were obviously going to take even longer than that. The guy either collected all manner of things for a whole variety of reasons, or he never threw *anything* away, or both (thought Duncan).

Give full credit for the answer (c): "or both."

In the desk, in various envelopes and folders, was almost every personal letter that Abraham Fetish had received (plus carbons of a lot of those he'd written) since he was about the age of twelve (the summer that his parents wrote that, although they missed him, they were really glad he was having such a wonderful time at camp and so proud that he had learned to do a jackknife dive *already*). It was at camp that he'd been convinced by an equally precocious twelve-year-old cabin mate that you never knew who was going to get famous, including yourself. ("Just imagine," David Dorfman'd told him, "all the stuff that people threw away. Little Billy Shakespeare's 'What I Did on My Summer Vacation' composition, for instance. What'd that be worth today? Or supposing you had a signed Al Einstein math homework where he said 7 was the square root of 34? Or what if whacky old Orville Wright's nephew had saved the postcard where his uncle wrote him: 'Don't tell your mother, but I'm thinking maybe I can fly!'?") The two of them (he and David) were, unsurprisingly, the only kids in camp who put carbon paper under their required weekly letters home.

So Duncan spent a lot of time first reading, and then scanning, such things as a report on Aunt Letitia's "bouts with old Si Attica (ha-ha)"; a carbon of the fourteen-year-old Fetish's confession to the thirteen-year-old Elizabeth Taylor that although he wasn't what he'd call "equestrial" himself, he loved to watch her "getting on and off a horse and everything in between"; and the assurance of the secretary of the Dean of Admissions at Harvard College that the Dean and the Committee would almost certainly "get" the various literary allusions in the candidate's Personal Statement. The only reference to drugs he came across was in a letter from someone named Ned who wrote "Dear A-Man" that he'd put two aspirins in his cola and thrown up.

A little after ten, Duncan got into the filing cabinets, and there discovered that Abraham Fetish had once been in the lumber business, had once been a stockbroker, had once opened a restaurant, and had once spent a week at a place called the Esalen Institute, at least partly as a result of his business experiences. There, he'd kept a rather lengthy journal, which Duncan had found . . . interesting. Up until he'd started in to read that journal, he'd thought that

self-awareness and personal growth were sort of soli-
tary enterprises, more studious and monkish, or even
tweedy than . . . er, well, athletic and group-cen-
tered and . . . *undressed*.

Duncan actually took that journal across the room
and sat down in an easy chair to read it, where the
light was better.

Terry knew the Fetish phone number, but not the
address so, when she landed at the Burlington Air-
port, she went and looked it up at a phone booth,
before she got in a cab.

The feelings of apprehension and uncertainty that
she'd had while flying had certainly not disappeared
on the ground. She was going to be arriving at this
address on South Willard Street at a time when (she
imagined) most Vermonters (weren't they almost all
farmers?) would have been asleep for a couple of
hours or so. She knew that Duncan's house was not a
farm, but. . . . Would there be a light on in the place?
Suppose there wasn't? Would she dare just lean on
the bell until somebody came and then tell whoever it
was (Silas? Martha?) that she *had to* see Duncan Banigan right away, on a matter of life and death? Suppose Silas and Martha told her to shove it? Or said
that he'd moved and they didn't know where? Her
baby-sitting-plus-part-time-checker-at-the-Shoprite
money had been, amazingly, enough for a round-trip
ticket on People Express, with some left over for
buses and cabs, and a little bit to eat on. But it
wouldn't stretch to a motel room. Would she just
have to turn around and fly back home? That would

be the worst, the absolute *pits*: to find that even with the best will in the world, she couldn't do the thing she felt was right; she couldn't stop whatever needed to be stopped, and let love conquer all.

She decided not even to think about that possibility until it came up. She was, for now, a girl — a *woman* — with a mission, and she was going to carry it through, carry it out — bring it off. She *could* make a difference; she *knew* she could. Like on *The A-Team*. It wasn't always some big "Them" who ended up on top.

But what, exactly — when (*not* if) she saw him — would she say to Duncan, just for openers?

As Abraham Fetish veered a little to the right, where Shelburne Road becomes South Willard Street, he was putting the finishing touches on the outline of a plan that had, as its Step One, a trip to his safe deposit box at the Howard Bank, the very first thing in the morning. Would it feel so very, very different to be . . . oh, say *Albert Farmer*, a fan of the Seattle Mariners, with season tickets for the Sonics (was it?) games? A man of quiet habits, many benefactions, who lived a cautious, peaceful life, working in the field of . . . *accident prevention*, yes.

Over and over again, in the course of the trip, he'd told himself to just stop thinking about the possibility of anything having happened to Caitlin. There were certain things in life that were, indeed, impossible to think about — *unthinkable* — even though they'd happened in the course of history, a lot of times before. And the deliberate killing of innocent beings was at the top of such a list. On top of *everybody's* list. It seemed so strange that *every* person in the world couldn't (therefore) take responsibility for his or her own peacefulness.

To just not *do* that, ever. Not start up.

He turned into the driveway by the Friends of Nukismetic Humanism House.

The last patient Lisle Hardaway had to look in on that evening was a man whose fractured wrist had needed surgery the day before. He'd been knocked over by a car while running across the street to the Bagel Bakery, and while he hadn't seen the guilty car — the thing had clipped him from the side and rear, and kept on going — he was quite certain it was driven by his former wife.

"When she heard I'd taken up swimming, and was building up my heart-lung system, she started to foam at the mouth," he confided to Lisle. "Her best friend told me. Just the *idea* I might outlive her — I'm eight years older, see? — was enough to drive her nuts. I doubt she was trying to kill me, actually — just slow my training down. You watch: I'll bet you anything she starts out in that new aerobic dancing class, next week. Well, I got news for her. As soon as I get this cast off, and you guys give me the go-ahead, I'm taking out a membership with Nautilus, or one of them. Maybe over in Essex some place, where there's no one she knows, where I could do it unobserved. Then, when she sees me at the club this summer, she'll turn fifteen shades of green, I guarantee you. I'll give *her* aerobics. And you know what else? I'm thinking of eating lots more natural foods, and cutting way back on the animal fats — how's that? Put some bucks into the body's natural defenses, via the vitamin route: stockpile a few antibodies, maybe. It'll be expensive as hell — shoot holes in my budget and all — but you gotta be alive to enjoy life, isn't that the truth now, doctor?"

"So far as we know," responded Doctor-almost Hardaway.

54. LAUNCH

When Mister Carlo heard some clock downtown begin to chime eleven, he decided it was time to make his move. As often is the case in life, his first step was the hardest; sitting on the stairs like that, his foot had gone to sleep. But still, he rose and staggered upwards, reached the top, and with painful feeling flooding back into his ankle, he limped out in the hallway on floor three. Duncan's door was just a few steps straight ahead, there on the right; he didn't hear a sound from any of the rooms on the entire corridor.

In his right hand Mister Carlo clutched his rolling pin. He'd coiled the rope and hung it on one shoulder; he'd put the pillow underneath that arm, the left one, and pressed it hard against his side. His left hand held the soap dish, with its chunky glob of peanut butter. He had to stoop and set it on the floor outside the door, before he used that hand to (very, very slowly) open it.

Sky woke up at once, of course. He sniffed. Mister Carlo put the pointed toe of one of his black shoes against the little plastic dish and pushed it; Sky smelled the peanut butter and the foot, both of them quite clearly. In his mind, neither one of them belonged there, in his room, though one of them (or something not unlike it) had been in before. Christopher sometimes had a snack, along with milk, at bedtime; said snack might very well include some ground-up something, nuts or beans, and Sky had never felt the need to bark at them. So, if Mister Carlo'd just backed out and shut the door and left the peanut butter in the room, the chances are that Sky would not have spoken. But when he didn't, when he stayed right there (waiting for his eyes to get adjusted to the dark), well, Sky objected, mildly.

"Woof," he said, or something very close to that.

And although Mister Carlo'd *known* a dog was going to be there, he was startled, anyway. The words *It's either him or me* blazed through his mind at rocket speed. He saw the bed in front of him, mounded by what had to be a sleeping human shape.

Whispering *nice doggie* toward the darkness to his right, Mister Carlo just took off: two steps, and then a leap, full length upon the bed. And even as he leaped, he struck.

Under him, the waterbed bucked forward, then surged back; it seemed (expectedly) to struggle; Mister Carlo'd never been aboard one in his life. He felt its motion and its warmth beneath him, sure enough, and in an energetic panic he pounded, pounded blindly with the rolling pin.

Sky started barking right away, of course, not little *woofs* this time, but full-scale *ruh-ruh-ruh-ruh-ruh's*.

Abraham Fetish was already inside the house when the barking started. He'd chosen to head down the first floor hall and take the back stairs up; no need for anyone to see him. His plan had been to head directly up to Caitlin's room, reassure himself about her safety, and then admit to her exactly all of what had happened in New Jersey and discuss with her such things as . . . well, Seattle, Tucson, possibly Barbados, Mozambique.

At first he thought the barking came from Caitlin's study (which *was* right under Duncan's room), but when he reached the second floor and realized it was coming from the third, now along with other sounds — the boy's voice, was that, hollering? — he kept on going up.

Terry Bissonette had just paid off her cab and gotten to the sidewalk out on Willard Street when Sky began the ruh-ruh-ruh-ing. She looked up at the house. It seemed to her the barks were coming from the . . . *third* floor, yes. She saw a light go on up there, and then another. It *could* be Duncan's dog, she thought, and hurried up the path. When she reached the front door, she took a deep breath and, instead of ringing, simply tried the door. The handle turned; she pushed; it opened. There was a staircase, wide and carpeted, in front of her. She hesitated, wondering if she should wait and ask directions, maybe. Then she told herself that that was *not* what Joan of Arc would do. And Wonderwoman didn't get her name from wondering.

She rocketed right up the stairs.

Caitlin hadn't exactly dozed off in her bedroom, as she waited for Duncan to come back from the movies; just spaced out a little. She probably heard the barking in her subconscious mind for ten or fifteen seconds before the wide-awake and conscious thoughts—That's Sky. Upstairs. He's barking—came to her. By the time she got to her feet and shook herself a little, she heard the sound of heavy footsteps steaming up the back, uncarpeted, wood stairs. *Elephantine* footsteps, even. She exited her room and started after them.

Duncan, logically enough, reacted first of all. Later on, he said it almost was as if a part of him was waiting for the sound — alert to it, at least — the way a mother might be to her baby's cry, a SAC commander to the ringing of a hotline. He burst on out the Fetish study door and up the big main staircase, three steps at a time.

From the doorway of his room, it appeared to him that Chris was being murdered. Without a thought, he dove (as he would for a loose ball) on top of . . .

277

well, whoever it might be, grabbing for the person's arms, his head, his weapon, shouting, "Cut it out, God damn it!"

Inasmuch as Sky, a savvy dog for sure but still a dog, didn't know how to turn on a lamp, the room was still dark (except for the light from the hall) when Abraham Fetish got there. A couple of doors on the corridor were just starting to open, and bearded Justin-types were peering out of them, but more in curiosity than anything. Nukismetic Humanists were not disposed to interfere too much; instead, they let fate run its course while they stood by, hoping to survive whatever happened — even profit by it, possibly. They clung to these beliefs even more strongly when it seemed, as in the present case, they might get hurt by an involvement.

"Yo!" cried Fetish to the writhing mass he saw atop the bed. Part of it was making sounds he recognized: exclamations in a foreign tongue (guesses, innuendoes, anatomical suggestions, and unlikelies).

And on top of Mister Carlo, almost certainly, was Duncan, who looked to have the little man *almost* wrapped up, but not completely, no. Who was under Carlo was impossible to tell. The best guess Fetish had was Christopher — but still, it *could* be Caitlin. Fetish, with the big man's knowledge of the pacifying usefulness of bulk, threw himself on top of Duncan.

When Caitlin got there, seconds later, and saw the now huge, rocking, rolling mass upon the bed, she ran and hit the light.

The first thing that she saw with total clarity was that her *father*, without doubt — why wasn't he in Clinton? — was the top layer of the pile.

"Daddy!" Caitlin yelled, and headed for the bed, thinking she might seize her father, drag him off, remove him from harm's way. That would be a start.

But Sky, still barking, somewhat in confusion, chose that moment, too, to make his own move toward the bed. He darted right in front of Caitlin, causing her to trip and pitch face forward on her father.

"Oof!" cried Fetish.

Duncan, having just then wrenched the rolling pin from Mister Carlo's hand, now twisted slightly out from under Fetish. With the light on, he could see exactly what the situation was. Christopher was nowhere on the bed, and he'd been sandwiched by the three of them, the three who he was (pretty) sure had planned and carried out his mother's and his brother's deaths.

All right, you bastards (Duncan thought) I'm not going to just let you do it to *me*. He raised the rolling pin.

"Duncan! Stop!" screamed Terry, from the door, bursting through a pack of bearded Friends. She launched herself directly at his arm and tried to grab the rolling pin in both her hands.

"Terry!" Duncan shouted, unbelievingly.

"Caitlin!" Fetish yelled. "You're safe!"

"Abe!" cried Mister Carlo. "*Get* him, for peace sake!"

JULIAN F. THOMPSON

"Oh, my God," moaned Caitlin, taking in the total mess and trying to figure out where this strange girl on top of her could possibly fit in.

"Ruh-ruh-ruh-ruh-ruh!" barked Sky. And (maybe) seeking to defuse the crisis facing him, he bit the waterbed.

55. THE FLOOD

To say it worked would be an understatement of a sort. Or, arguably, even a mistake. Looked at from a certain point of view, nothing can be said to work that brings about destruction on so grand a scale. I mean, you wouldn't want to say the Chicago Fire worked, now would you? Or the San Francisco Earthquake? Or some other major incidents in history that both of us might mention, although neither of us will, all right?

Then, looked at another way — as you remember Duncan often did, or *used to*, I should say — one can always make the argument that nothing *really* works at all. Even jogging, bathing, and what-have-you. People drop dead doing all of those, most every day.

But, being fair, you also *should* point out that the destruction, though extremely great — irreparable, in part — was very, *very* highly localized (one ancient waterbed). And if you looked at the whole occurrence from the point of view expressed (and acted on) by Terry and Caitlin both, at different times: that every one of us *can* work, take charge of our own lives, and maybe even play a part in causing peace and sanity, Sky's action was a great success. The people on that bed were on the brink before he bit it; he had done the only thing he could to maybe wash them off it.

For with that bite, well, water just exploded from the thing — that punctured bag (which just a tick before was Christopher's so greatly prized, though used-and-bargain-priced-at-a-garage-sale, early 1967 model waterbed).

Not only did the water from it dampen anybody's homicidal plans who might have had them, it also made them think of other things: breathing (in the case of Mister Carlo) and how strange their wet, warm clothing felt; when they'd last been in a bath with other people. For here they seemed to be, a pile made up of one huge red-faced balding man, two pretty girls, a tiny Spanish-looking guy, a lanky high school athlete; they looked at one another and they felt . . . well, in a word, ridiculous.

Embarrassed, does that mean? Why surely.

Relieved, as well? Why not.

The dog was perfectly delighted. He pranced around the bed, splashing in an inch or so of water, wiggling his body and waggling his tail. His bark was different, softer, slower, very close to "Ha — Ha — Ha."

The Friends, absurdly, leaped this way and that, onto Duncan's bed, atop both dressers and the chairs, trying to keep their feet from getting wet. For all they knew, what they'd been looking at was not a *fight* ("for gosh sakes") but just a friendly roughhouse of some sort. They felt no fallout whatsoever.

56. DISCONTINUED

It was Abraham Fetish, ever the improviser, always with a way with words, who got them out of there — the principals, that is. He also organized, cajoled the Friends so that they started (laughing merrily) to mop and bail and wring things out, before the downstairs ceilings fell.

And finally, after a few minutes' pause for toweling off and changing, he brought the other five of them (one dog) together in his study, where he closed and locked the door.

"It's time for everyone to know the truth," he said. "Of course, I don't mean 'everyone' — far from it." He looked at Terry. "I take it you're a friend of Duncan's?" Terry nodded. "From New Jersey?" She bobbed her head again. He turned to Duncan. "You feel she should hear this?"

"Yes." He didn't hesitate.

Abraham Fetish cleared his throat and started.

Terry looked bewildered for a while, then horrified; Duncan: grim; Mister Carlo: fugitive; Sky: delighted (still); Abraham himself: both burdened and determined.

As her father told the story, Caitlin Fetish wept.

When he was finished, no one moved, at first. The story seemed to fill the room with hopelessness: People are a certain way, and always will be. There weren't any questions; everything was clear enough.

Duncan Banigan stood up and looked around at all of them.

"I don't know what's meant to happen now," he said. "What I feel is — *seems* like — just too much for anyone to feel at once. I guess I understand what happened in New Jersey, now — and up here, too. I'm glad I finally know the truth."

He looked at Mister Carlo.

"I guess I hate you for doing . . . *that*." His voice cracked on the word. "And it'll always seem to me you didn't have to."

"And you . . . ," he said to Abraham, and shook his head, and made a gesture of dismissal with his arm: a flat-hand, overhanded wave.

He never looked at Caitlin.

"But what am I meant to *do*?" He turned to Terry, then. "Am I meant to want to see them all dead, too?

Or put in cages for a lot of years? Should I want that? Is that some kind of answer?"

Abraham Fetish was sitting with his legs and arms crossed, his chin bowed down on his chest; Mister Carlo was leaning forward with his knees apart, his fingers laced together, staring at the floor. But Caitlin, dry-eyed, raised her head and looked at Duncan.

Terry, too, was looking straight at him. He was asking her, but also not. He knew. But she knew *him*. Better than . . . well, anyone. He wanted her to say he had it right.

"Not for you," she said.

Duncan let his breath out, nodded.

"So let's us just go home," he said, and smiled a sweet, sad smile at her, and Sky.

The men sat frozen in their chairs and so did Caitlin Fetish. She didn't think that she could bear it if he didn't know she'd never lied to him, but once — that all the rest of it had been the truth. But why should he believe her if she told him now? And anyway, that play was over and the game was going on: Telling him might be the ultimate in selfishness, her final little ego trip. She held her breath, determined not to cry again before he left.

As Duncan passed behind her chair, he touched her, very lightly, on the shoulder with his fingertips. He touched her much the way he might have touched a teammate who had lost the ball, or made a foul, or missed an easy lay-up shot. And, blessedly, he also kept on going.

ABOUT THE AUTHOR

Julian F. Thompson lives here and there in Vermont with his wife Polly, who is a painter and designer. He is the author of four other novels, *A Band of Angels* (also available from Scholastic), *A Question of Survival*, *Facing It*, and *The Grounding of Group 6*.